COCONUT MILK CASUALTY

CLAIRE'S CANDLES - BOOK 3

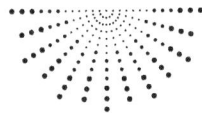

AGATHA FROST

Published by Pink Tree Publishing Limited in 2020

All characters and events in this publication, other than those clearly in the public domain, are fictitious and any resemblance to real persons, living or dead, is purely coincidental.

Copyright © Pink Tree Publishing Limited.

The moral right of the author has been asserted.

All rights reserved. This book or any portion thereof may not be reproduced or used in any manner whatsoever without the express written permission of the publisher except for the use of brief quotations in a book review.

For questions and comments about this book, please contact pinktreepublishing@gmail.com

www.pinktreepublishing.com
www.agathafrost.com

WANT TO BE KEPT UP TO DATE WITH AGATHA FROST RELEASES? *SIGN UP THE FREE NEWSLETTER!*

www.AgathaFrost.com

You can also follow **Agatha Frost** across social media. Search 'Agatha Frost' on:

Facebook
Twitter
Goodreads
Instagram

ALSO BY AGATHA FROST

Claire's Candles

1. Vanilla Bean Vengeance
2. Black Cherry Betrayal
3. Coconut Milk Casualty
4. Rose Petal Revenge (NEW!)

Peridale Cafe

Book 1-10 Boxset

1. Pancakes and Corpses
2. Lemonade and Lies
3. Doughnuts and Deception
4. Chocolate Cake and Chaos
5. Shortbread and Sorrow
6. Espresso and Evil
7. Macarons and Mayhem
8. Fruit Cake and Fear
9. Birthday Cake and Bodies
10. Gingerbread and Ghosts

11. Cupcakes and Casualties
12. Blueberry Muffins and Misfortune
13. Ice Cream and Incidents
14. Champagne and Catastrophes
15. Wedding Cake and Woes
16. Red Velvet and Revenge
17. Vegetables and Vengeance
18. Cheesecake and Confusion
19. Brownies and Bloodshed
20. Cocktails and Cowardice
21. Profiteroles and Poison
22. Pudding and Poison (NEW!)

INTRODUCTION FROM AGATHA FROST

Hello there! Welcome to another installment of my ***Claire's Candles Cozy Mystery*** series! If this is a return visit to Northash, welcome back, and if this is your first visit, *welcome*! Since this is the third book in a series with overlapping subplots, I recommend reading the first and second books in the series, ***Vanilla Bean Vengeance*** and ***Black Cherry Betrayal***, although the mystery in this story can be enjoyed as a standalone (and I never leave a mystery hanging).

Another note: I am British, and Claire's Candles is set in the North West of England. Depending on where you live, you may come across words/phrases you don't understand, or might think are spelt wrong (we love throwing the 'u' into words like 'colour'). If that's the case, I hope you enjoy experiencing something a little different, although I believe that anyone speaking any variety of English will be able to enjoy this book, and isn't reading all about learning?

Please*, *enjoy! And when you're finished, don't forget to leave a review on Amazon (they help, a lot), and to check out my other series, Peridale Cafe, which has over 20 cozy adventures for you to enjoy!

CHAPTER ONE

*R*yan was stalling her. For the last twenty minutes, Claire had been perched on the edge of his bed, watching him pick out a shirt like his life depended on it, and yet he still hadn't settled on one.

"We're only going to the pub for a drink," she pointed out. "You're not meeting the Queen."

"It's a special night." He pulled a blue shirt out of the small wardrobe, assessed it, and put it straight back. "We're celebrating."

Claire's stomach rolled like a barrel even as the corners of her lips pricked up into a smile. After months of delays and preparation (and unfortunately, a dead body in the attic), in the morning, her dream candle shop would open its doors for the first time.

Nerves had riddled her for weeks, but that hadn't stopped excitement fizzing alongside them like a child's anticipation on Christmas Eve.

"It's only The Hesketh Arms," she said, looking down at her simple outfit of a plain black t-shirt and a pair of slightly ripped, fitted jeans. "A pint at the pub the night before I open, you said."

"*This* one." He pulled out a short-sleeved shirt on a hanger. "I like this one."

"That's the first one you picked."

"Is it?" He held the white shirt at arm's length and gave it a shake. "Just needs a little iron, and we'll be on our way."

Claire assessed Ryan as he kicked up the small ironing board in the cramped room. He hadn't looked her in the eyes since he'd planted her on the bed, and his cheeks flushed red every time she tried to hurry him. She'd known him since they were toddlers, and in the more than thirty years that had passed since then, he'd never learned to lie convincingly. It wouldn't take much interrogation to crack him, but for now, she'd play along out of sheer curiosity.

"Still no luck finding a house?" she asked as she looked around the dated bed and breakfast bedroom.

"The rental property market in Northash has as much flow as the duck pond at Starfall Park." He climbed over a suitcase and a pile of black bags to grab the iron off the windowsill. "Well, the houses in *my* price range, at least. As much as I'd love a four-bedroom detached cottage with a country view, the gym doesn't pay *that* well. I keep searching, but nobody ever seems to leave this place."

Being a quiet, sleepy village with expansive country views, decent shopping, good schools close by, a large factory for employment, and a gorgeous public park, Northash had been the perfect place for families to flock to for generations. By this point, most of the village's residents had been there since birth and weren't in a rush to leave.

"You left," she reminded him, the words catching unexpectedly in the back of her throat.

"And yet here I am." He filled the kettle with water at the small sink in the corner of the bedroom, a grin lifting his freckled cheeks. "As glad as I am to be back home, I wish it were as easy to find places here as it was in Spain." He sighed. "Although, that was probably because Maya's family were so well connected. She had a cousin or an uncle in every sector, I swear."

Ryan laid out the shirt on the ironing board and attempted to mask his sadness with a half-smile, but Claire knew him better than that. Though much had changed in the long years without contact, Claire had never lost her urge to protect him. When she saw the familiar pained look in his eyes as he stared at the heating iron, she only wanted to shield him more.

Ryan only looked like that when he mentioned Maya. Maya had lured Ryan away from Northash. He met her on a lad's holiday when he was eighteen and rushed off to Spain to live with her without seeming to give it much thought. At the time, he'd only told Claire that Maya was beautiful and he had fallen in love with her. Claire lost more than a friend the day Ryan left.

"The perfect house is waiting around the corner," Claire assured him, not wanting to let the conversation linger in the sadness of the past. "But seriously, if we don't set off soon, it'll be standing room only. You know what the pub is like on Friday nights."

Steam hissed from the tiny holes as he ran the hot plate of the iron along every crease with military precision, flipping the shirt this way and that to attack it from every angle. Clearly, he wasn't in any rush.

"I suppose I'm going to have to start ironing my own stuff when I move out," she mused aloud. "As it stands, I never have the chance. My mother washes, dries, shrinks, irons, and puts away my clothes before I even wake up."

"Your mother is of a different breed."

"I'll tell her you said that."

"The second you want to start putting up the flat's furniture, let me know," he said, turning the shirt to work on the collar.

"I will." A yawn quivered Claire's lips before ripping her mouth fully open. "Right after I get the shop opening out of the way. I haven't had a second to think about the flat."

"*Done!*" he announced, swishing the shirt off the board. "Throw me that deodorant can on my dresser, would you?"

Claire rolled back onto the soft double bed and plucked the deodorant from the cluttered bedside. She was pleased to see four of her recent candle prototypes that she'd given him for opinions, each burned to a different degree. She'd spent months getting her stock levels to a point she felt comfortable to open with, but she never stopped developing new scents when she had the time. Ryan seemed to love every candle she gave him to test, and while it wasn't as helpful as the constructive criticism she pulled from her family, she loved that he wanted to be involved in the process.

When she turned back and tossed him the can, he'd already whipped off the tight t-shirt he'd worn during his long shift at the gym. While he casually misted his armpits with the minty pressurised spray, her gaze fell on his washboard abs. She didn't know where else to look, so she let herself linger there. She'd had months to accept that he wasn't the little dumpling he'd been when he left. She was sure it would take another few years to fully accept the Adonis body he had somehow chiselled from the fluffy softness she remembered. Claire's softness was still very much soft, and she had no desire to start chipping away at it.

"Jeans, next," he said as he buttoned up the crisp, short-sleeved shirt. "Won't take two—"

"These." Claire plucked a pair of skinny black jeans from the scrunched up pile of clothing on the bed. "They're tight enough that they don't need ironing. You look good in them."

"I do?"

"Sure." Cheeks hot, she tossed them across the room. "Chop-chop."

Ryan caught the jeans and looked as though he was going to argue his right to spend the next half an hour umming and ahhing over every pair of trousers he owned. Claire left her seat on the bed and waited by the door. Determined not to stare at the backs of his muscled legs as he wriggled into the jeans, her eyes landed on a plastic bag jammed into the corner by the wardrobe. Bundled-together paintbrushes, some dirty with paint, poked out through the handle hole. Claire nudged the bag with her foot, revealing dozens of tubes of watercolour paints inside. A few had been opened, but most of the tubes were plump and unsqueezed. From this angle, she could see a tall wooden easel stuffed in the gap between the old mahogany wardrobe and the wood-chip wallpaper. Just as she shifted to see if a painting was attached, Ryan appeared between her and the wardrobe, fully dressed, the scent of his sweet aftershave thick in the air.

"Are you painting again?" she asked, trying to step around him. "Let me have a look."

"It's nothing," he said, his pale cheeks flushing the deepest red before he turned her around to face the door. "C'mon, let's go."

She pursed her lips. "*Now* you want to rush?"

"I'm just trying it out again." He closed the door firmly and twisted the key in the lock. "I haven't painted in a while. Not since Mum died." He forced the key into the tight pocket of his jeans and clapped his hands together before saying, "You're right. The pub will be packed if we take any longer."

Ryan hurried down the floral hallway and bounced down the stairs, forcing Claire to follow. She wanted to push the subject, to see his work, but she could wait until Ryan was ready to talk about it, even if she did feel a little pushed out. Ryan had painted all through his childhood and teen years, and back then, Claire was always the first person to whom he showed his works in progress.

Rather than leaving the B&B straight away, Ryan went to the doorway of the sitting room. Agnes and Jeanie, the twin sisters who owned the place, swayed in opposite rocking chairs, knitting. Nine-year-old Amelia coloured violently in a book at the coffee table, showing no care for the patterns or lines. Hugo, the quieter of the two at seven-years-old, was curled up in an armchair next to Jeanie, his face buried in his beloved handheld games console.

If Ryan had a distinct look when he talked about Maya, he wore the opposite when he looked at his children. It reminded Claire of the way she looked at her cats when she caught them snuggled up at the bottom of the bed in the morning.

"Thanks again for watching them," Ryan said, patting the doorframe to get the sisters' attention. "I won't be out too late."

"It's no bother," Jeanie said, grinning over her knitting. "Always happy to help."

"It's like running a nursery," Agnes said, her tone bitter and less jovial than her sister's.

"Take your time." Jeanie shook her head at Agnes with slightly pursed lips. "They're no bother, honestly.

Keeps me on my toes. You've been our only guests for a while, so you have our full attention."

Agnes rolled her eyes and looped the wool forcefully over one of the needles. Slightly under her breath, she muttered, "Speak for yourself."

"Can we come?" Amelia whined without looking up from her colouring book. "It's *boring* here."

"I could put the television on?" Jeanie suggested.

"No *Netflix*," she moaned. "What's the point?"

"What about a card game? Or dominos?"

"Don't want to."

Agnes jabbed her needle into the next stitch. "Children are so ungrateful these days."

"Behave yourself," Ryan commanded, including them both but focusing his finger on Amelia. "I *mean* it. I don't want a repeat of last time."

"Fiiine," Amelia huffed, switching from a red pencil crayon to a green one. "I just wanted to see what would happen. It was Hugo's idea anyway."

"Was not."

"The fish were quite fine after we returned them to the tank," Jeanie said with a soft chuckle, shooting her sister a sharp look obviously intended to keep Agnes from uttering further complaints. "Kids will be kids. Now, go and enjoy the party!"

Before Claire could say a word, Ryan pulled her

away from the sitting room and steered her down the hall to the front door.

"*Party?*"

"What?"

"She just said 'enjoy the party!'"

"Did she?"

"Ryan . . ." Claire held onto the doorframe before he could push her out. "Did my mother put you up to this?"

"It was supposed to be a surprise." He exhaled, sounding a mixture of relieved and disappointed. "It was supposed to start at seven. Your dad sent me a text and told me to stall for half an hour."

"And picking out shirts was all you could think of?"

"Worked, didn't it?" He smiled a little. "Just try and act as surprised as you can because I think your mother might kill me if she finds out. She's been planning this all week."

"Don't worry," Claire said, looping her arm through his, "I have my drama GCSE to fall back on."

"Didn't you get a D?"

"Details."

As they walked the short distance from the bed and breakfast to the village square under the last of the late spring sun, Claire couldn't be anything but excited. Unmarried, childless, and, until recently, a simple factory worker, she had always felt like a failure when it came to her mother's exacting standards, not that she'd ever actively tried to reach them. Only since acquiring the shop had she seen regular glimmers of pride in her mother's eyes. Usually, Claire hated surprises, and parties in her honour were always the last thing she wanted to do to celebrate any occasion, but she was touched her mother had gone to such lengths.

"We're just going for a quiet drink at the pub, okay?" Ryan said firmly, pausing on the corner before they entered the square. "Everyone will be there, and they're all going to be staring directly at you. Crack, and they'll see it. You need to muster all the acting skills that come with a D in GCSE drama."

"I'll try my best." She cracked her knuckles as she twisted her neck side to side. "Mr Jenkins will wish he cast me as Little Red Riding Hood in the Year Ten play."

"Who did you end up playing?"

"One of the three little pigs."

"In Red Riding Hood?"

"It was remixed," she said. "I'd rather not go into it. I'm still scarred from opening night. I forgot my lines and—"

"Your costume caught on one of the wooden trees,"

he said, his eyes lighting up as he slapped her on the arm with the back of his hand, "and you pulled down half the set!"

"Like I said," she said, cheeks flushing crimson, "I don't want to talk about it."

Linking arms again, they entered the village's central square. The setting sun bled orange into the sky over The Hesketh Arms. The clock tower in the centre let them know it was twenty-five minutes to eight. The shops were long since closed; even the gym Ryan managed only stayed open until half-past six. The lack of shops to browse or weights to lift, however, didn't mean the square was empty. The beer garden in front of The Hesketh Arms was packed out in the warm, twilit evening, and Claire imagined the garden at the rear, next to the canal, was even busier.

Amongst the faces, Claire spotted two of her closest friends: Sally, an estate agent she'd known as long as Ryan, and Damon, whom she'd worked alongside in the Warton Candle Factory for years until she was unceremoniously fired earlier in the year.

"Not much of a surprise," Claire muttered as she waved.

Sally spotted her and returned a hand, but with none of the vigour expected for such an occasion. It took Claire a moment to realise Sally and Damon, while next to each other, were both staring silently into the square in the same direction.

Claire followed their eyelines directly to her shop, Claire's Candles, where she found her mother and father, and Granny Greta. Em, another of her friends and one of Ryan's colleagues at the gym, was also there. Unlike Sally and Damon, they weren't standing around staring.

"*Come on!*" cried Claire's mother, Janet, dunking a brush into a soapy mop bucket before slapping it against the panelled bay window. While it certainly wasn't odd to see her mother cleaning things, she never did so while wearing the navy-blue pantsuit reserved for special occasions. "She's going to be here any second, and it's not coming off!"

Em caught Claire's eye and cleared her throat. Janet let the brush drop and stepped aside, letting Claire see why her father had implored Ryan to delay her at the B&B. Red paint, smeared like blood, covered the front of her shop, spreading from the far edge of the window and past the door before spilling onto Wilson's Green Grocer's on one side and The Abbey Fryer fish and chip shop on the other.

Claire slipped away from Ryan and walked closer, and Em met her halfway. The yoga instructor wrapped her hand tight around Claire's and squeezed with all her might. Granny Greta turned, her nails in her mouth—a bad habit in times of stress that she'd passed on to Claire. Her father, Alan nudged Janet, and they looked at her with a shared apology in their eyes.

Claire wanted to speak, to ask what had happened, but it became apparent when she reached the road directly in front of her shop.

The paint wasn't smeared at all.

It was very intentional.

A single word sprayed in red.

CONGRATULATIONS.

CHAPTER TWO

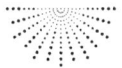

*T*he next morning, alone in the flat above the shop, Claire peeled back the net curtain in the front window. The long hand of the clock tower ticked a minute closer to nine.

Eight minutes until her life changed forever.

Biting her lip, Claire let out a quivering breath as she peered at the tops of the heads gathered by the front door. Considering the string of bad luck that had followed the shop as of late, she was surprised to see anyone at all, let alone a small crowd.

"*Claire?*" her mother called up the staircase. "It's almost time."

Turning away from the window, Claire crossed the box-cluttered flat to the small bathroom. Flicking on the light in the salmon-coloured restroom, she glanced at the hatch in the ceiling. The position of the attic door was strange, but no stranger than what she'd found up there. On the day Sally handed over the keys, a foul smell had taken them up to the attic, where they'd found the body of Jane Brindle, the former occupant of the shop and the flat.

There'd been a time not long before discovering Jane's body when Claire's most significant worry had been finding the money to secure the shop. Still, as it turned out, that had been the easiest part. As though uncovering a crime scene wasn't enough, the fuse box exploded less than a week after solving the murderous plot that had left Jane's body in the attic.

When the electrician came in to fix the box, he found the family of mice that had chewed through the wires and caused the explosion. The entire downstairs needed a full re-wiring, destroying Claire's decorating in the process. Then, the same day she finished patching up the paintwork after the plasterer left, a bad storm blew half the tiles off the roof.

Each roadblock had been challenging to deal with, but seventeen years stagnating on the production line in the local candle factory had awoken a determination within her. Her mother claimed Claire was cursed, but

Claire didn't believe in such things. After all, as bad as her luck seemed to be, the various misfortunes were all merely happening *around* her, not to her.

Until the graffiti.

Pushing any thought of curses to the back of her mind, she stepped into the bathroom and assessed her reflection in the mirror. She'd had her thin, mousy bob freshly cut to her jaw last week, and had even picked up some new plastic clear-frame glasses at her latest eye appointment two days ago. Thankfully, her comically bad eyesight hadn't worsened (for another year at least).

"*Little one?*" This call came from her father.

"One second."

Claire took a final look in the mirror. She dusted off the last of the crumbs from the rushed bacon sandwich she'd wolfed down at her parents' cottage before hurrying down to the shop to finish the final preparations. She left the bathroom and flicked off the light before walking slowly down the dark, narrow staircase, equally thrilled and terrified that the moment was so close after so much waiting.

In the kitchen filled with the stock that didn't fit on the shelves, her mother and father greeted her with identical frozen, uncertain smiles. Granny Greta was behind them, her Yorkshire Terrier, Spud, at her feet. Her smile, at least, was more relaxed and supportive.

Janet gave her outfit a quick scan. For one of the few times in Claire's life, she didn't comment, despite spending much of the last fortnight trying to drag Claire to Marks & Spencer's to buy clothes that 'looked the part,' whatever that meant. After briefly toying with the idea of wearing a uniform, Claire had plumbed for a dark-green, scoop-neck t-shirt with slightly rolled sleeves and a pair of ripped, fitted grey jeans, both purchased from the local second-hand shop. Since hers was the name above the door, she intended to kick things off by simply being herself. Besides, she'd spent seventeen years shackled to the awful uniforms at the factory.

"It's not too late, you know," Janet said, dragging Claire out of sight of the open doorway. "They'll all come back next week. You don't have to do this."

"They'll understand," Alan added.

"The graffiti is gone," Claire reminded them, pushing forward her brightest smile. "Your pressure washer made sure of that."

"That's the spirit!" Greta shuffled forward with Spud and gave Claire a little hug. "You're a Harris woman, and we don't back down to bullies! It was probably just some kids messing around." She glanced at Janet. "*Your* advert in the paper probably cottoned them on to the opening."

Claire crouched to stroke Spud, and he immediately began nibbling her fingers. She didn't mind though; she'd rather be out of the firing line that happened whenever her mother and grandmother were in the same room.

"Oh, it would be *my* fault," Janet snapped, throwing her hands up before planting them solidly on her narrow hips. "It's not just about the graffiti, Greta. It's *clearly* a threat! A *message*! What if someone wants to . . . wants to . . . kill—"

"That's *more* than enough, Janet!" Greta's voice boomed from her short, broad frame, a finger firm in her daughter-in-law's face. "You're going to get the poor girl worked up, and for what? She's already made up her mind!" She peered around Janet. "What do you say, Alan?"

"Claire, your mother is right," he said, his weary gaze on the floor. "I don't feel comfortable with this. If it were anyone else, I'd say the same things. A couple more days, and DI Ramsbottom and the team might have a chance to get to the bottom of it."

"The only thing DI Ramsbottom can get to the

bottom of is a bag of crisps," said Greta, shaking her head. "Claire, what do you *want*? If you want to close – rather, not open – I'll clear everyone off in seconds. Just say the word."

Leaving Spud to chase his tail, Claire walked over to the doorway. The mere sight of her ready-and-waiting shop sent a tingle down her spine. She hadn't been able to see them from her vantage point in the flat above, but Sally and Damon were at the very front of the crowd, staring quietly in opposite directions. Much as she wanted them to get along, she still hadn't figured out a way to bring two of her closest friends closer. Still, they were both there to support her, making the thought of facing the crowd an easier one.

Beyond them, two uniformed police officers were loitering by the clock tower. They could have been on break, but Claire wouldn't have been surprised if her father had asked them to watch out. Detective Inspector Alan Harris might have retired, but he still had enough respect at the station to make something happen with one phone call. He'd never admit to it, so she wouldn't ask, but just seeing their uniforms eased her mind further.

"We've all waited a long time for this day," Claire said, her voice firm. "I'm opening."

"Good girl!" Greta clapped.

"But they could be out there *right now!*" Janet peered around the edge of the doorway. "Waiting to pounce on you at any moment! Oh, Claire. *Who* have you upset?"

"Don't blame the girl, Janet!" Greta shook her head. "Honestly, you don't half know how to put your foot in it."

"It's fine, Gran," Claire said, eager to avoid more bickering. "I was up half the night trying to answer that question, and I couldn't come up with anything. I also decided it doesn't matter. Not today, at least."

"But it's not just—"

"Mother." Claire rested a hand on Janet's shoulder. "This is my dream, remember? I'm opening that door in" – she paused and tilted her head to look at her mother's wristwatch – "three minutes, and if a sniper is waiting in the clock tower to shoot me down, so be it."

"*Claire!*" Janet cried, slapping her arm. "You mustn't joke about such things!"

But Claire's bad-taste joke made Alan chuckle, which caused Janet to join in. Claire was glad of a little laughter after such a serious twelve or so hours. Alan pulled them both into a hug, and there they remained until a frenzied knocking at the front door pulled Claire away.

"Come on, mate!" Sally called through the front door, her phone up to the glass. "It's nine!"

Claire's stomach lurched, and, for a moment, she thought she might throw up. But as she steadied herself, a wide, authentic smile connected from ear to ear. She looked around for Granny Greta, but she seemed to have slipped out the slightly open back door while Claire had been enveloped in a parental hug.

Leaving her parents alone in the kitchen, Claire walked through the doorway and into the shop. Before heading straight to the door, she rested her hands on the counter and took in her hard work.

The walls were cool grey with matching linoleum wood flooring, a perfect backdrop for her candles. Jars of all shapes, sizes, and colours lined the walls on the flatpack shelves Ryan had helped assemble, backlit by warm LED strip lighting. In the centre, a large, circular display unit made of natural wood – a second-hand find from Em – featured the first 'Star Candle of the Month.'

Claire's father had helped her assemble the simple counter – albeit without the instructions. The front panel was supposed to be a sparkling, glossy white instead of exposed raw chipboard. Still, by the time any of them realised their mistake, Claire had already grown fond of the contrast. A flatscreen electric till took up half the counter, preloaded with her stock levels and ready to keep track of her inventory. It had a drawer for petty cash, and was connected to her phone for card transactions – Sally's suggestion; they used a similar system at the estate agents up the road where she worked. In the bay window, distressed wooden boxes of all heights taken from the local butcher's thanks to Damon's father being the owner, displayed a dozen of the summer scents ready for the season's official start the following day.

To Claire, it was as perfect as it was ever going to get. Despite how much bad luck had been thrown her way, she was ready to share her dream with the village she loved.

She walked over to the door.

She flipped the sign.

She twisted the lock.

Focusing on Sally and Damon through the glass, she opened Claire's Candles for the first time. Behind her, a champagne cork flew at the ceiling, and the small crowd gave a little cheer.

"About time, I'd say!" Sally applauded. "Congratulations, mate. You actually pulled this—"

Sally's voice trailed off, and she pressed to the side

as Granny Greta forced her way over the threshold, Spud in her arms.

"There was no way I wasn't going to be your shop's first customer!" she announced, patting Claire's cheek as she passed. "And don't let anyone near that till until I've filled my basket. I'm going to be your first paying customer too!"

The crowd chuckled, clearly amused by Claire's gran's antics.

"Figured it out?" Sally asked quietly in her ear as she gave her a quick hug.

Claire shook her head but couldn't linger on the question.

One by one, the waiting crowd loaded into the shop, each person offering congratulations. Some even bore gifts. Damon gave her a card signed by everyone at the factory, but he had to get to a shift so he couldn't stay. Marley and Eugene from the café around the corner gave her a bouquet of red roses, Theresa and Malcolm from the pub offered a bottle of champagne, Walter and Wendy from the greengrocer's next door settled a fruit basket on the counter, and more than a handful of people gave her cards echoing their verbal congratulations.

While her mother and father mingled and handed

out flutes of champagne, Claire positioned herself by the counter and observed her full shop. At present, most of her customers were her fellow shopkeepers showing their support, but that didn't stop them filling their baskets. Each time someone picked a candle off the shelf and inhaled deeply, Claire's chest tingled. Even if they put it back, the excitement remained.

"They all smell divine, Claire," Greta said as she dumped a full basket on the counter. "Ring me up, and don't forget the receipt!"

Thanks to Sally teaching her how to use the system over several bottles of red wine the previous weekend, Claire whizzed through the six candles her gran had chosen with ease and loaded them straight into a brown paper bag with a black flame emblem printed on the side. Greta insisted Claire charge her full price, but she tapped 'Friends and Family Discount' anyway, which took the price down to just above what it cost Claire to make the candles.

"I love my new bank card," Greta said as she tapped it against the small card portal on the counter. "No more fiddly PINs! I could never get used to them after the switch from signing. But this! One tap and I'm away."

The machine printed out the first receipt. Claire

ripped it off with a satisfying tear and joked, "Receipt okay in the bag, madame?"

"I think it will be." Greta winked playfully before leaning in and saying, "I'm so proud of you, you know. I always knew you'd get here."

"Thanks, Gran," she said, returning the smile. "I'm proud of myself."

Greta and Spud were the first to leave. Before long, a small queue formed at the counter. Claire rang them through with ease, only having to call on Sally once to show her how to delete an item she accidentally scanned twice.

Once Sally had to leave to get to a house viewing, and Janet left for her shift in the post office two doors down, Claire noticed she was no longer serving her fellow shopkeepers, but real customers. Claire didn't know if they'd come for the opening or just wandered in, but by lunchtime, half the shelves were bare. Before she had a chance to figure out how she was going to fill them while manning the counter, her father emerged from the kitchen, pushing a box with his good foot. He began restocking the central 'Star Candle of the Month' display with jars of her latest summery coconut milk creation.

Though Marley and Eugene's café would be packed by noon, the lunch hour gave Claire's shop room to breathe. The steady flow of the morning dwindled to only a couple of casual browsers. She'd planned to use any downtime to restock, but her father had almost finished filling the last few gaps in the popular vanilla row.

"You've taken to this like a duck to water," Alan said, patting her on the shoulder as he kicked an empty cardboard box along the floor into the kitchen. "I knew you would."

Claire glanced out the window. The two police officers hadn't budged from the clock tower all morning. They'd long since stopped trying to look like they weren't on watch and now actively stared directly at, and only at, Claire's Candles. And as much as she loved having her father with her on such a special day, she didn't think his persistent presence was by accident. He rarely spent much time away from his potting shed at the bottom of the garden these days. Not since a brain tumour forced him to retire from the force, and the removal of which caused nerve damage, giving a limp on his left side.

"I know you're scared, Dad," she said, joining him in the kitchen when the last of the customers left. "Should I be?"

Without looking up at her, he continued making himself a cup of tea at the small drinks station she'd set up in the corner. His avoidance of her eyes was all the answer she needed. After a morning of being too distracted to think about it, her mind went straight back to the graffiti, and more importantly, who could have left it.

"It's peculiar, I'll say that," he said, pouring a drop of milk into his cup. "Let's just see what DI Ramsbottom finds out."

Harry Ramsbottom and her father had worked together at the local station for years, with Harry ascending from DS to DI when Alan had to bow out. In the short time he'd been the village's detective inspector, he'd blundered several cases and, according to local gossip, was hanging on by a thread. Everyone, including her father, knew Alan was the better DI – possibly the best the village had ever had.

"Dad?" she said quietly, stepping closer. "Is there something you're not telling me?"

Picking up his tea, Alan turned and plastered on his fakest smile as he leaned against the counter. He lifted the hot tea to his lips and blew on it before taking a sip. Claire knew him well enough to know he always waited for his tea to cool down before he sipped, and for the second time in two days, she felt she was being stalled.

"What makes you ask that?"

"It's just," she started, pausing to consider her words carefully, "you seem confident in Harry's skills all of a sudden, which makes me wonder if there's something you know that I don't."

Alan sipped the hot tea again, grimacing this time from his lack of blowing. The shop door opened behind her, but she didn't turn away from her father.

"Customers," he said, shuffling off with his tea. "Can't keep them waiting."

Irked by his aloof manner, Claire followed her father back into the shop, although her mood immediately picked up when she saw Ryan. He'd promised he'd come in during his lunch break, although he hadn't mentioned he'd be bringing flowers. He stepped fully into the shop, revealing Em right behind him. Both were in their work clothes from the gym, although they were very different outfits. Ryan wore one of the revealing vests that left more of his muscles uncovered than not and a pair of baggy grey shorts. Em, on the other hand, wore rainbow tie-dye joggers with a baggy orange tunic. The colours brought out the contrast of her skin, entirely inked.

"Just stopped by the local graveyard," he said with a grin as he passed her the colourful bouquet.

"He did not!" Em said, pulling Claire into a tight

hug. "He spent a considerable amount of time picking them out from the florists, actually."

"He's like that with shirts," Claire said, returning the grin. "Good timing. You missed the rush."

"Don't get used to it," Ryan said. "It's the same at the gym. Once everyone fills their bellies, it's back to shopping."

Alan took the flowers from Ryan and shuffled back into the kitchen to add them to the plastic cups they were using in place of vases until they could take the several bouquets home.

"I hardly recognise this place as my mum's tearoom," Em said with no hint of sadness as she looked around the place. "You've done a terrific job. I imagine that if my mother were still here with us, and after she got over the shock, she'd have loved what you've done with the place."

Claire reached around the counter and pulled out the gift she'd wrapped last night and put there this morning. She handed it to Em, whose eyes widened almost comically.

"I think I'm the one meant to give you a gift," Em said, one hand resting on her chest as she accepted the present. She ripped back the paper, exposing the small sample of blue floral wallpaper Claire had salvaged from the tearoom walls and framed during the decorating process. "Claire..."

"I know you never wanted to run this tearoom," Claire said, looking around and unable to see any trace of it beyond the general shape, "but I thought maybe a little memento would—"

"It's perfect." Em smiled, tears welling in her eyes. "Thank you." She reached into her pocket and pulled out a small red velvet box. "Since we're giving gifts, I might as well give you this now."

Claire accepted the box from Em, who had fast become someone she spent a lot of her time with. They'd always known each other enough to offer a vague greeting, but solving the murder of Jane, Em's mother, had bonded them in a way Claire couldn't explain. With Em being a fifty-year-old self-confessed hippie with a bald head and tattoos, they couldn't have been more different, but Claire loved her. Em had a way of making Claire feel free and special whenever they were together. Claire opened the box with a snap, and a gold flame on a gold chain shone up at her from its bed of red velvet.

"Em, I..."

"I think it's just costume jewellery," Em said as she scooped it out of the box and walked around Claire to fix it around her neck, "but when I saw it, I immediately thought of you."

Claire let the cold metal settle against her chest before pulling it out from behind her t-shirt to rest on the fabric. She'd never been one for jewellery, and yet already she couldn't think of a reason to ever take it off.

"I get it," Ryan said, nodding at it with his hands on his hips. "Candles."

"And who said men weren't smart?" Em said, giving Claire's shoulders a little squeeze. "I'll leave you two alone. Ryan had something he wanted to ask you."

"He does?" Claire spun around and stared at Em, who could only offer a shrug and a cheeky smile. "Well, I'm sure I can take a little break."

"Go on." Em nodded at the door. "I've seen half the women at the gym with your little brown bags this morning. You've earned a bit of fresh air. I'm sure your father and I can look after this place."

"Oh, yes," Alan said as he returned with his tea. "Take as long as you need. I'm sure we'll manage."

Em wrapped her arm around Alan and gave him a small hug, and though Claire wasn't keen on the idea of leaving her shop so soon, she was more than a little curious to find out what Ryan had to say. She followed him out of the shop into the bright afternoon sun.

As they headed quickly towards the gym, which had taken over the old library building on the other side of the square, the police officers leaning against the clock tower responded to something on their walkies. For a moment, she dreaded the thought that her father had asked them to tail her, but they cut across the square and went in the direction of the church. Claire let out a sigh of relief.

Pumping pop music playing on the TVs inside the gym greeted them as the automatic doors slid open. A couple of women chatted as they lazily cycled on bikes, and a lone man checked himself out in the mirror, baring his teeth as he pumped the heavy-looking weight. Em had already laid out her yoga corner, but her next class didn't start for a few hours.

"I could have shown you on my phone," Ryan said as he walked behind the glass counter, "but I didn't want your dad to see. I know he's not in the police anymore, but I didn't want him to add two and two if I've got this wrong."

"About what?"

"This." He tapped the spacebar on the keyboard and turned the computer screen to face her. "I completely forgot about this until I saw him again this morning. Don't know the fella, but he comes in often, and given his height, he's not hard to miss."

Claire squinted at a grainy video taken from what appeared to be a camera in the men's locker room. Before she could ask what on earth Ryan was trying to show her, one of the cubicle doors opened, and an incredibly tall, muscular man walked out with a half-open backpack slung over his shoulder. As he resettled the backpack, a flash of silver fell out. He scooped it up casually, and it was back in his bag in an instant. He zipped up the backpack and looked around, his eyes homing in on the camera long enough for Claire to recognise his face. The tall man walked under the camera and out of view, and seconds later, Ryan emerged from another cubicle in the clothes he'd been wearing when Claire had arrived at the B&B yesterday.

"I remember hearing the sound and thinking it sounded like someone had dropped an empty can of beer or something." Ryan tapped the spacebar to pause the video. "I thought 'someone's keen to start their Friday night early.'" He rewound the clip back to the can falling out of the man's bag. "Could be a coincidence, but that looks like spray paint to me. I only caught the back of him as he left. I knew he was the same guy when I saw him this morning because of the sheer size of the fella."

"He's six foot six," she said, almost under her breath.

"You can tell that just from looking at him?"

"I know him." Her mouth was dry as sandpaper. "He's called Nicholas Bates. Everyone calls him Nick. He works at the candle factory."

"The factory?" Ryan recoiled, and he frowned. "What if it wasn't him?"

"It was."

Rather than try to explain it to Ryan, Claire left the gym and set off across the square, her heart thumping in her chest. She felt dizzy, but never in her life had she been more certain of something. She felt Ryan rushing after her, but the anger and frustration bubbling up in her spirit welled in her eyes. She rubbed away the tears, angry at herself for letting *that* man make her cry again.

She hurried past Trinity Community Church, ignoring the wedding taking place. There was another small square, Christ Church Square, directly behind it. It was made up of nine terraced cottages in three rows of three, with the back wall around the church completing the square. Rather than a clock tower commanding attention in the centre, there was a small car park with a sign demanding that it was for 'Residents Only – No Exceptions.'

Christ Church Square was a quiet, closed-off part of the village, seen as a desirable place to live for those who couldn't stretch to the luxury of one of Northash's many detached cottages. Today, however, the usual quiet was nowhere to be found.

Claire stopped on the corner, her heart shuddering when she saw an elderly woman sobbing in front of the slightly open door of the very cottage she'd been heading for. One of the police officers who had been outside Claire's shop all day was attempting to calm the woman. Presumably the other was inside, dealing with the source of the woman's screaming.

"Claire." Ryan grabbed her forcefully and shook her until their eyes met; fear filled his green gaze. "What is going on? Who is this man, and why would he want to scare you like that?"

Claire tried to speak, but nothing came. Neighbours were emerging from their homes to see what was causing all the noise, but Claire could only stare at the howling woman. Somehow, someway, she had a strong feeling about what was behind that door.

Her legs kicked into gear and she left Ryan almost without realising what she was doing. The neighbours, a mixture of people at least sixty and older, flocked to the woman.

"What is it, Geraldine?" asked the first woman to reach the sobbing woman's side. "You're screaming the entire square down."

"It's *Nick*!" Geraldine cried, clutching the woman's shoulders as though to hold herself up. "I was walking past. I just happened to look in and . . . and . . ." She paused, clutching her throat. "He was just hanging there, a rope around his neck."

"*What?*" the neighbour cried.

As the rest of the neighbours reacted in similar disbelief, Claire stumbled to a stop and gazed through the open door.

There, at the end of the hall, a long, muscular frame hung suspended from the ceiling. She turned away and straight into Ryan's chest. He wrapped his arms around her and squeezed.

"Oh God," he said, pulling her away from the door to a bench on the edge of the square. "Claire, what is happening? Why would Nick want to do this?"

"He didn't," she said, wiping away a stray tear, "he was put up to it."

"By whom?"

"This was *his* house," she said, nodding at the cottage, but unable to look at it. "They were housemates."

"Whose house?"

Claire gulped, more angry tears filling her eyes. This time, Ryan used the pad of his thumb to banish them before she could even blink. The second police officer walked out, and with a single shake of his head confirmed what they all knew.

"My Uncle Pat," she said, her throat closing around the name. "He was the one congratulating me."

"Why?"

"To get my attention," she said, her unblinking gaze fixed on the cobbled road, "and it worked."

CHAPTER THREE

The ambulance arrived, but Claire couldn't stand the thought of staying to watch things unfold. She walked back to her shop in such shock, she didn't realise she was clenching Ryan's hand until she was back in the safety of Claire's Candles and finally released it.

Two people were browsing separately, inhaling the various scents, and another waited at the counter. At that moment, Claire didn't care whether they liked her candles. She never thought she'd long for an empty shop on opening day, and yet she wouldn't have been upset if they'd left without paying for anything.

"We figured it out!" Alan said with a chuckle, one finger on the side of his face while another hovered over the till's screen. "It took us a minute, but we got there in the end." He beamed at the woman who was buying three large coconut milk jars and a handful of clean linen scented melts, and said, "Cash or card, madame?"

"Card, please."

"*Card.*" He gave the screen a confident stab. "Do the tap thing when you're ready."

While the woman dug out her card, Em loaded the three candles, and the wax melts into one of the flame-emblem bags. Her eyes remained fixed on Claire, the firmness of her gaze clearly seeing right through the façade of calmness Claire was feigning for her customers' benefit. One of the men walked out without buying anything, and before the door finished closing behind him, Claire flipped the sign to 'CLOSED' to prevent the post-lunch rush Ryan had warned her of. The woman at the counter paid and accepted her bag, with the final customer taking her place just as quickly. By the time she'd paid and was on her way out, Alan's expression mirrored Em's.

"*Claire?*" He rushed around, clinging to the counter and already reaching for the display unit to keep his balance. "What is it? What's happened, little one?"

"Did you know it was *him*?" Claire asked, her tone blunter than she'd ever usually take with her father.

"Did you know Uncle Pat was behind what happened to my shop last night?"

Alan winced, his head going to the side as though her words had slapped him across the face. He gritted his jaw and clenched his eyes shut. "Claire, please . . ."

"Nicholas Bates is dead," she announced as calmly as she could. "Hanged himself, by the sounds of it." She ducked to meet her father's eyes and rested a hand on his shoulder. "Dad, did you have a feeling *he* was behind the graffiti somehow?"

Alan nodded.

"Ryan has footage of Nick at the gym, dropping a can that looks suspiciously like spray paint," she said, looking at Em, who appeared the most shocked of them all. "I think *he* convinced Nick to do it. And now, Nick is dead. I can't think of a single reason he'd want to vandalise my shop . . . but his former roommate? We both know . . ."

Claire's voice trailed off to nothing; she could not bear creating more pain in her father's eyes – pain he'd been hiding since the day he had to listen to his younger brother confess to murdering Nicola Warton and Jeff Lang. All this time, it had been there, barely under the surface. Claire had known it would come out eventually.

She wrapped her arms around her father and held

him tightly. She wanted to tell him she knew about the letters Uncle Pat had sent her from prison. He'd been pilfering and hiding them in his potting shed for a while, and she'd only happened to stumble on them by accident. The confession was on the tip of her tongue, but she couldn't bring herself to say such a thing in front of an audience. Even if that audience was Em.

"I" – Em rushed around the counter, her eyes wide – "I need to go."

"Did you know him?" Ryan asked, opening the door for her.

"Very well," she said with a nod. "He's – *was* – my good friend Ste's brother. He can't hear about this in the wind. It needs to come from someone he trusts. I need to go to him."

Em left the shop, already at a full sprint by the time she passed the window. Claire imagined she was going straight to the Northash Taxi rank across from the park. Claire had met Ste briefly; Em had introduced him as a good friend from her high school days back in the eighties.

Claire guided her father onto the small stool behind the counter. He sat down and clutched her hand as though the roles had reversed and she was the parent.

"This doesn't make any sense," Ryan said, squinting

at the floor. "He was in the gym just over an hour ago. I *saw* him. That's how I remembered hearing the can. He was working out . . . he was laughing . . . he seemed *fine*."

Claire knew enough about suicide to recognise it wasn't as simple as laughing or not laughing, but something about the events following last night's paint discovery didn't sit right with her. If Nick had acted on Uncle Pat's instructions, could it be a coincidence that he chose the day after his act of vandalism to take his life?

Through the window, she spotted DI Ramsbottom walking across the square. Leaving her father's side, she hurried towards him. Despite her own low-level of fitness, she crossed the distance more easily than he. DI Ramsbottom was a large, lumbering man in clothes that barely fit, with a shiny golden toupee Claire had seen resist the strongest wind.

"Detective Inspector?" she called as soon as she was in range. "Have you just come from Nick's house?"

"You heard already?" He stopped and looked around the square. "How quickly do things spread around here?"

"I was in the wrong place at the right time. Or maybe the wrong place at the wrong time." Dropping her voice, she asked, "I don't suppose you found a red can of spray paint in there? Perhaps in a gym bag or the bin?"

"You think it was him?" Ramsbottom frowned. "Whatever for?"

"I'll take that as a no." She looked around the square as shoppers went about their day – only a couple of shocked faces surfaced the sea of ignorance. "If you find anything, can you let me know?"

"Of course," he said as his frown deepened, "but I have to ask, why the sudden interest in Nick? Did you know him? Because if you did, I'd like to ask . . ." His voice trailed off, and he clicked his fingers together. "*Of course*! Your uncle! They shared that very cottage, didn't they? Do you think Pat could have put him up to it?"

"Possibly." She glanced at the gym. "If you speak to Ryan Tyler, he'll show you a video of Nick with a can of spray paint."

DI Ramsbottom patted down his pockets. He pulled half a packet of crisps from one before retrieving a pen and small notepad from the other. He scribbled down the name and nodded at Claire as though to thank her for the tip.

"I don't suppose you've visited your uncle since he was banged up?"

"No," she said quickly. "No communication."

"That'd do it." He nodded, evidently putting the pieces together more slowly than Claire had. "Well, I'd say that's as good as a case solved. I'll look out for the spray paint, but first, I need to get to Lilac Gifts." He hooked his thumb over his shoulder at the card and gift shop on the row of shops adjacent to Claire's. "I need to tell Gwyneth. She's my niece, and she's had an on and off thing with Nick for far longer than I care to acknowledge." He leaned in, and in a lower voice, admitted, "Between you and me, I always knew the only way they were ever going to be fully off was if he moved away or died. Looks like it was the latter."

Before Claire could ask any questions about why he wouldn't want Nick Bates romantically involved with his niece, DI Ramsbottom hobbled off to the small shop. Claire squinted through the window. Gwyneth was behind the counter. Around the same age as Em and Ste, Gwyneth was often referred to as the 'Marilyn of Northash' thanks to her trademark white curls and dark beauty mark. Claire turned towards her shop, not wanting to witness the delivery of such harrowing news.

"I need to get back to the gym," Ryan said when she walked back in, though his tone made it clear he wished he could stay. "I've already gone five over my break."

"Go on," Claire said, smiling her appreciation. "We'll talk when you're finished."

Ryan pulled her into a hug, and for the first time since they were teenagers, gave her forehead a little kiss. He left, and even with all the day's chaos, Claire's lips turned up in the briefest of smiles.

"Why does the sign say *closed*?" Janet cried as she hurried into the shop with a plastic bag. "I packed us some lovely salads for lunch. Thought it might be nice if we all ate together for a change."

Janet dumped the bag on the counter and got to work unloading her Tupperware and cutlery. She opened the lids before looking at Alan, and saying, "Don't sulk, dear. I'll make fish and chips for dinner, my special way. The less deep-fried food we eat at our age, the—"

"Mum," Claire cut her off. "I think we should all go home. There's a lot we need to talk about. A man has died."

"*Who?*" she replied curtly. "What man?"

"Nick Bates."

"Oh." Janet looked down at the salads as if she no longer recognised them before returning them to the bag. "Good idea, dear. We'll . . . we'll just eat these at home."

CHAPTER FOUR

Claire's decision to open the shop on Saturday was a purposeful one. Most of the out-of-town shoppers travelled in on Saturdays, usually to spend time in Starfall Park before wandering around the many independent shops the village had to offer. For Claire, the timing worked out perfectly. Her first half-day of sales had covered the overheads for at least another week, with enough left over to finally order some new fragrance oils after depleting her stores while readying the shop's inventory.

Subconsciously perhaps, Claire had known she'd immediately need a day off after the emotions of opening day. She had expected to be exhausted from standing all day, but she hadn't factored a graffiti message and a death into her decision making. Her mind and emotions were far more wearied than her legs, and she'd never been more grateful for Northash honouring the tradition closing shops on Sundays.

"I really don't want to go out," Alan said as Janet pushed him down the hallway. "I'm not in the mood."

"Your shoes are already on!" Janet exclaimed, grabbing the car keys from the hook on the wall before opening the front door. "You love going to the garden centre."

"But *today* of *all* days?"

"I need the fresh air."

"We live in the countryside!"

"Only the other day you were complaining about needing some of that stuff to make the grass greener." Janet pushed him over the threshold, grabbing his cane from beside the door because he never would. "Go and get yourself settled in the car."

"If we're going," he said, reaching back and snatching the keys from her, "I'm driving. I want to get there and back today."

"I'm a perfectly fine driver!"

"Perfectly fine, yes," he said, turning to wave goodbye to Claire, "if you're judging by a snail's standards."

From where Claire was leaning against the counter in the kitchen, she returned the wave and smiled as much as she could muster. When her father was in the car, her mother hurried down the hallway, all pretence dropped from her expression.

"Whatever you're up to," she said, extending a long, slender finger, "you better tell me when I get back. Your father is having a bad foot day, so forcing me to get him out of the house had better be important."

"It is," Claire assured her, straight-faced. "I promise I'll tell you."

Claire left off 'when you get back,' but she wasn't sure her mother would turn and leave if she said, 'when the time is right.' Thankfully, Janet didn't catch on, and after one final purse of her lips, she left, closing the front door behind her.

When the rumble of the car engine faded out of the sleepy cul-de-sac, Claire hurried out the back door and down the garden path under a blanket of thick grey clouds. She didn't make a habit of hiding things from her parents, nor did she enjoy sneaking around behind her father's back, but he hadn't left her much choice. She slipped into the small shed and went straight to the top drawer of his potting desk.

One eye closed, she pulled open the drawer. She let out a breath, glad to see the letters, but that relief quickly turned to horror. The first time she'd stumbled across the pile of sealed envelopes, there'd been six.

Last time she'd checked, there'd been nine. Now, well over a dozen were heaped in the drawer, with the one on top dated four days ago.

"What do you want?" she asked as she scooped them out.

Letters crammed under her arm, Claire left the shed. After closing the door, she made eyes with Graham over the garden fence. He gave her a tight smile and a little wave as he loaded a black bag into the outdoor bin. She nodded and returned her neighbour's smile, though considering whose words she had under her arm, she couldn't bear to stay and chat. Despite the state of his marriage to Nicola, she was still his wife when Uncle Pat pushed her to her death in the factory.

Once back in the kitchen, she dumped the letters on the island before pulling the roller blind over the window. She wasn't sure Graham could see her, and even if he could, how he'd manage to read the tiny writing. Still, she didn't want to take the risk of him seeing her reaction to whatever was contained within the letters.

Heart pounding, she stared at the mound. All were addressed to her in her uncle's handwriting, and yet the guilt at taking them from the shed was almost too much to bear. Her father had been stealing her mail for a while, rushing to the doormat to fish out any letters sent from Her Majesty's Prison Manchester before she had a chance to see them. She'd wanted to talk to him about it since she'd found them in the shed, but the subject wasn't an easy one to approach.

Domino sauntered into the kitchen and jumped up onto the island. She walked around the edge and headbutted Claire as though she knew she needed some support. Claire picked her up and gave her a little cuddle, which Domino briefly allowed before wriggling away. Sid was the cuddlier of her two cats, but the giant grey fluffball was no doubt curled up on her bed, sound asleep.

The front door opened, and Sally let herself in, her phone sandwiched between her ear and shoulder. Domino darted from the kitchen and back upstairs with steps as loud as a small child's. Sally watched the cat as she waved to Claire, closing the door with her hip.

"Yes," she said into the phone, rolling her eyes with a sigh. "I understand, Mr Folkston, but it's Sunday, and the office is closed. Yes, I do have keys. No, I'm going to go to the office to look at the paperwork. Yes, I'm aware of your budget, but The Manse will still be on the market tomorrow morning. Because it's my one day off!"

Sally hung up and tossed her phone onto the

counter before dropping a white paper bag onto the marble. Hands in her hair, she gave herself a moment to let out a frustrated grumble before sliding onto one of the stools. Claire filled a large pan with water and placed it on the hob before turning it on to boil.

"That's the *last* time I give my personal number to a client," she said, reaching into the bag to pull out a giant box of assorted pastries. "They think because they're spending a small fortune I should be on call twenty-four hours a day."

"I don't know how you do it." Claire plucked a sugar-coated jam-filled doughnut from the box.

"Commission," she said before biting into a glazed yum-yum. "It's a great motivator."

"Where did you get these from?"

"There's a little bakery over in Downham that opens Sundays," she said, taking another bite. "After everything you told me on the phone, it's the least I could do." Her eyes drifted to the kitchen island. "Are they all from *him*?"

"Every single one."

"Bloody hell, Claire," she mumbled, licking the icing off her lips before taking another bite. "How have you not ripped them all open, knowing where they were?"

"Because I love my father," she said, glancing at the

blinds and imagining his shed at the bottom of the garden, "and he wouldn't be stealing my mail if he didn't think he was doing the right thing."

"Have you asked him why he's doing it?"

"I know *why* he's doing it. He's trying to protect me from whatever Pat has to say."

"Your uncle murdering two people will do that," she said, plucking one of the fat doughnuts from the box. "It would have driven me crazy, though. I was always that kid who read the last page of a book first to see how it would end. I couldn't stand not knowing."

A knock at the back door startled them both. Damon cupped his hands against the window and peered in. Behind him, the heavy clouds were beginning to release the first droplets of the day's forecasted rain. Claire opened the back door.

"Sorry, I'm late," he said, panting slightly as he walked into the kitchen. "I was playing *Dawn Ship 2*, and I lost track of time."

Damon smiled stiffly at Sally before sitting at the breakfast bar, leaving a seat between them. She returned the smile, but neither vocalised a greeting. Not for the first – or even the five-hundredth – time, Claire wished she could figure out a way to get them to like each other as much as she liked them both. The answer eluded her, though she supposed she was grateful they so often agreed to be in the same room, if only for her sake. Still, Sally nudged the box over to Damon, and he accepted a glazed cinnamon roll.

"Are these *the* letters?" Damon mumbled through a mouthful.

Claire nodded as she flicked the kettle on.

"It's not going to take three of us to rip open a small pile of letters," Sally said, checking her phone, which already had a fresh string of notifications filling the screen.

"We're not *ripping* them open." Claire opened the cupboard under the sink and pulled out the iron, its cord neatly wrapped up. "We're going to steam them open. I need to be able to put them back without my dad knowing, and if he has his way, they won't be out for long."

"All this to avoid talking to your dad about your uncle?" Sally laughed, still distracted by her phone. "Claire . . . really?"

"I'm not avoiding it." She could barely look at her friend. "He is. After what happened to Nick yesterday, I closed my shop and sat my mum and dad down at the dining room table. Dad lasted two minutes before he locked himself in the shed." Guilt stabbed in her chest. "I wish he'd talk to me about it, but I love him enough not to force him into this conversation until he's ready."

"What if he's never ready?"

"He will be," Claire said hopefully, plugging the iron into the socket on the breakfast bar, next to Sally. "But I can't wait. I need to know what my uncle wants."

"And you really think he put Nick up to spraying the front of your shop?" Damon asked.

"Yes." Claire pulled out her phone to show them the recording Ryan had sent her that morning. "Ramsbottom thinks it's as good as solved."

"And now Nick's dead, and you'll never know for sure," Sally said, wide-eyed as she stared at the phone. "Isn't it always strange when someone you vaguely know dies? I'm sad, but didn't *know* know him, you know? I dealt with him a little when your uncle went to prison. We manage the property he rents – *rented*. Just the other month, he finally came in to sign the documents that fully transferred the tenancy into his name. Seemed pleasant enough. Built like a brick house."

"I worked with him on deliveries when I first started at the factory," Damon said, picking at his nails. "I thought driving around in the vans would be more interesting than working on the production line, but I couldn't stand the early mornings and never being in one place. And, truth be told, I didn't like working with him. He seemed normal enough at first, but he was *weird*."

"In what way?" Claire asked.

"He scared me," he said, scrunching up his face as he stared blankly in the direction of the letters. "He'd so easily brag about the awful things he did when he was my age. At the time, I was nineteen, and he was about thirty, so there was a bit of a gap. Maybe I was young and didn't understand his humour."

"What kinds of things?" Sally asked, addressing Damon for the first time.

"He used to break into people's cars and joyride them around the village," he said. "Stories about robbing houses, that sort of thing. I'm older now than he was back then, and I can't imagine laughing about doing stuff like that in my teen years, but maybe that's just my shyness." He paused to push up his glasses. "Old William transferred me immediately. He was always good like that."

"And that's when we re-connected at the stickers station," Claire said fondly. "What you've said lines up with how DI Ramsbottom acted when he told me his niece was involved with Nick. He practically said he was glad the guy was dead."

"No one will challenge a guy that big and

muscular," Sally said with a wistful sigh. "Should we get on with peeling open these letters? I suppose you want us to keep an eye out for mentions of Nick?"

"And my shop."

"I'll take the hob," Damon said, hopping off the stool before sliding the iron to Sally. "This is almost exciting."

After steaming it over the kettle, Claire eased open the first envelope with a little help from a butter knife. As she pulled out the letter, a knot formed in her throat at the sight of her uncle's familiar, neat handwriting filling two sides of lined A4 office paper.

Turning it the correct way up, Claire inhaled and read:

June 5th

It's me again. I understand why you're not responding; I really do. That's if you're even receiving these. I feel like I'm talking to myself right now. I fear the guards may be destroying my mail before it has a chance to leave the prison. Alas, I'll keep trying. Even if no one is reading these, I need to talk to someone. To say I am going crazy in here would be an understatement. The cell feels smaller each day, the conversations more repetitive, the food somehow blander. Yesterday, we had bubble and squeak for the fourth day in a row. I never thought I'd miss my mother's cooking. Give my love to Granny Greta.

Claire paused and pulled her thumb from her mouth, not knowing when she'd started nibbling on the nail. After spending so long ignoring her curiosity, the raw honesty of her uncle's words shocked her. She continued reading from the top:

The days are long and slow. I spend most of my time reading in the library. I don't fit in, and they know that. There are others who don't fit in, but we've yet to become friends. Everyone is scared. I'm scared. I'm living amongst some of the worst in society, and yet, I know I, too, am one of them. I'll never be able to repay my debt, I know that. This is my punishment. I understand, but the thought of doing this with no contact from my family – from you – makes the days almost unbearable.

Once again, I've attached a visiting order in the hopes you change your mind.

It's still me, Claire. I promise.

Uncle Pat

"I feel sick." Claire leaned against the counter, clutching the letter so hard it scrunched in her palm. "Any mention of the shop or Nick?"

Sally looked up and shook her head. "There's a visiting order attached to this one for last month."

"This one too." Damon held up a small piece of card. "From two weeks ago. Are you sure you want us to read these?"

"Yeah, this is pretty deep," Sally said as she turned her letter over. "It sounds like he's really struggling in there."

"Keep reading."

Claire cycled through three more letters, all of them similar in content. They were almost word for word identical, with the levels of apology and begging increasing or decreasing depending on how recently they'd been sent. Claire waited to feel something, but nothing penetrated the shroud of numbness.

"I'm not even the one he needs to beg for forgiveness," she said almost to herself after finishing another letter. Her gaze drifted to the tiles above the oven, precisely where Graham's cottage sat next door. "I'm not the victim of what he did."

"You're the victim of the vandalism," Sally pointed out. "But I still haven't seen any mention of your shop."

"Me neither," Damon said. "Although he seems to be sick of eating potatoes with every . . ."

Damon's voice trailed off as he turned his ear towards the door with a slight squint in his eyes. Claire heard the familiar rumble of an engine seconds later. Leaving her final letter on the side, she rushed into the hallway and pulled back the curtain. Through the light shower of rain, her father's rear headlights reversed onto the driveway.

"No, no, *no!*" she cried, hurrying back into the kitchen. "They're back already. What do we do?"

"I don't know!" Sally cried, jumping up. "Maybe let him walk in and see?"

"And admit I was sneaking around behind his back?"

"He's been sneaking behind yours, mate." Sally stuffed one of the letters back in its envelope and slapped down the still sticky glue along the flap. "These are addressed to you. You have every right to open them."

"Stall him." Damon pushed Claire into the hallway. "We'll figure it out."

He closed the kitchen door behind her, leaving her to wait in the hallway until the car doors slammed. Through the net curtains, she watched her mother hurry up the path, her face as panicked as Claire felt.

"It was bloody *closed!*" Janet hissed when she opened the front door. "One of the water mains burst and flooded the damn road in front of it. I tried to get him to another, but he wasn't having any of it." She looked around Claire's shoulder at the closed kitchen door. "What's going on in there?"

"I'll explain later," she said, immediately pushing forward a smile as her father hobbled up the path with his cane. "No luck?"

"Burst pipe," he said, obviously relieved. "I'll go sometime in the week."

"Shame you didn't get to have lunch there," she said, leaning against the doorframe. "Why don't we go into the village? I heard The Park Inn has a new food menu that's meant to be half decent."

"And overpriced."

"The Hesketh Arms, then?" Claire reached for her denim jacket. "I could just murder a pint of Hesketh Homebrew."

"I'm really not in the mood, little one," he said, mustering a weary smile before pushing past her. "I just want to sit down and put my feet up with the crossword."

Claire held her breath as he walked down the hallway, knowing she couldn't say more without completely giving herself away. She hurried after him, hovering in his shadow and preparing to explain herself. He opened the door and shuffled in.

"You win!" Sally cried from the dining room table.

A board of *Scrabble* between her and Damon. "I'm rubbish at this."

"*Scrabble?*" Janet arched a brow, her lips pursing as she scanned the kitchen. "You were playing board games?"

"My idea." Damon held up his hands. "Can't get enough of it."

Claire looked around the kitchen, but the envelopes had gone. The iron was still out, but the stove was off, and the pot was upturned on the draining board next to the sink. Alan went straight to the kettle and pulled out enough cups for everyone.

"I should get going," Sally announced, standing and nodding for Damon to do the same. "I'll give you a lift into the village since it's raining."

"Right," Damon said, rising. "I have that thing I need to do anyway."

"I'll show you out," Claire said, already following them into the hallway.

Leaving her parents in the kitchen, she closed the door. A trio of audible sighs escaped as they made their way to the front door. Sally pulled it open, the rain thickening by the second.

"I put them back in the shed," Damon whispered as he hugged her goodbye. "Top drawer, like you said."

"Thank you," she whispered back. "I owe you one."

Sally and Damon climbed into Sally's parked car on the edge of the cul-de-sac. Claire waved them off into the rain and waited until they'd gone before returning to the kitchen. Alan had put two of the cups away and was now making two cups of tea, and a cup of coffee for Claire. Claire slipped into one of the chairs at the dining room table and tried not to let her frustration and confusion register too much on her face.

"All the words are gibberish," said Alan as he set a cup of coffee in front of her, tilting his head at the beige letter tiles on the board.

"You know what Damon is like." Claire picked up the board and dumped the pieces back into the box before cramming it in the dining room console table. "He insisted we play by his weird internet rules. No wonder he won."

Alan nodded that he understood, but Claire knew she couldn't get anything past him. As much as his limp had physically slowed him down, and as forgetful as he could be since the operation, his inner detective was as active as ever. She didn't mind him thinking she was up to something as long as he didn't figure out exactly what. Much as she'd insisted her father was the one not ready to have the awkward Uncle Pat conversation, the more she thought about it, neither was she.

"I think I'll have this in my shed," he said, already hobbling to the back door with the assistance of the furniture, his cane – as always – abandoned by the front door. "I need to have my new bedding flowers ready for when the rain eases."

"Going to last all week, apparently," Janet called as she cranked up the blind over the kitchen window. "So much for the first day of summer."

"Typical *British* summer," Alan said with a half-hearted chuckle as he opened the door. "I'll be back in for dinner."

Janet waited until Alan was shut in his shed before marching across the kitchen. Before she reached Claire, her eyes went to something on the floor and being the neat freak that she was, she picked it up. Claire immediately recognised it as one of the postcard-sized visiting orders from Pat's letter.

"Polling card," she said, snatching it off her mother before she could get a closer look.

"But there's no election coming up." Janet folded her arms, one brow peaking up her forehead. "Claire, if you don't tell me what's going on right now, I swear, I'll – I'll—"

"Send me to bed without supper?"

"I'm *warning* you, Claire!" Janet planted one hand

on the counter before her gaze went to the end of the breakfast bar. "*Why* is the iron out?"

"I needed to iron something."

"And here was me thinking you didn't know how."

Before the barrage of questions came, Claire adopted one of her father's avoidance techniques and locked herself in the small water closet under the stairs. Sitting on the toilet lid, she pulled the visiting order from her pocket and unfolded it. It must have fallen out of one of the letters, and just by chance, it must have fallen out of the letter he sent four days ago. The visiting order was in two days.

The thought of visiting Uncle Pat in prison had crossed her mind, but each time, she'd dismissed it without a second thought. She didn't want to go and see him, nor did she want to hear him out as desperately as he seemed to want her to.

But her mind went to Nick. She didn't know him enough to say he hadn't killed himself, and yet the disconcerted feeling that had settled over her when he was found dead in the cottage he used to share with her uncle had yet to ease. The feeling in her chest only itched more with each new titbit she gleaned from people's perceptions of the deceased man.

Flushing the toilet, she pushed the visiting order back into her pocket, knowing what she had to do.

CHAPTER FIVE

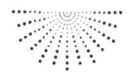

*B*reakfast the next morning was so awkward it made Claire wish she had prioritised setting up the flat above her shop. As much as she had loved temporarily living with her parents, at thirty-five, she felt too old to be walking around on eggshells.

Alan silently wolfed down a bowl of cornflakes while the promised rain poured outside. Janet did the same, glaring at him the whole time as her spoon forcefully hit the bottom of her bowl. When they were both finished, they went their separate ways, leaving Claire to load the breakfast things into the dishwasher. Her parents had bickered late into the night. Even though her bedroom shared a wall with their master suite, she hadn't been able to make out the specifics – not that it was difficult to assume the subject.

Rain or not, Claire didn't consider asking her mother for a lift into the village. They'd driven in together on Saturday, but the post office's new limited opening times had slashed Janet's Monday shift off the schedule for the first time in her near-forty years of employment. Though she had promised to take Claire into the village on Mondays regardless, Claire preferred the rain over another awkward silence; the humid air was thick enough.

After packing a change of clothes and a fresh pair of shoes into a plastic bag, she pulled on her father's large raincoat. The hood hung way over her eyes, but it kept the rain out like nothing else. Her mother's raincoat was more for show – not that it would fit Claire anyway. Alan's smelt like him, forcing her to think about him alone in the shed at the bottom of the garden. She wanted to go to him, to make things better, but she couldn't think of a way to do it without making things worse. After adding her handbag to the plastic bag, Claire knotted it and left without so much as a goodbye.

Head down and bag held tightly in her hand, Claire set off straight into the cul-de-sac. The rain fell thick and fast, but there was no wind to alter its course to the ground. Summer-warmed rain made for a far less unpleasant walk than the same journey come wintertime.

The opening of the lane into the village appeared in no time, and it wasn't long before she reached the bridge over the canal. When she did, headlights shone from behind, forcing her to the side of the road. The car pulled up next to her, and the door opened. As he had done many times before, Graham motioned for Claire to get into the car.

"You should have knocked for me," he said, offering a smile. He set off as soon as she'd fastened her seatbelt. "I knew spring had been far too kind to us. We're paying for it in buckets by the looks of the forecast."

"And here I thought my coconut milk candle would be perfect for the season," she said, lowering her hood. "If only there was a way to develop a rain-scented candle. I'd probably make a fortune."

Graham offered a laugh, but Claire didn't detect much humour in it. The awkwardness she had been hoping to avoid with her mother now hung in the air, albeit for different reasons.

Not terribly long ago, she and Graham had simply been neighbours, knowing each other enough only to nod and smile. Claire hadn't even known his wife,

Nicola – who eventually became her boss – until her death. As a couple, Graham and Nicola had kept themselves to themselves, and Janet stopped trying to invite them to her annual garden barbeques after they ignored three in a row.

Graham had been the one to make right his wife's theft of Claire's vanilla candle formula at the factory. That money had become the deposit on the shop.

Nicola's death, however, had stitched their paths together before that. Not only had Claire suspected (and accused) Graham of the murders her uncle had committed, Graham had misguidedly attempted to kiss her at the same time he and Sally were having an affair during a break in her marriage.

The water under the bridge was too deep for there not to be awkwardness.

"How was the opening?" he asked, breaking a minute-long silence. "Sorry I couldn't get down. Those Saturday shifts at the factory have really taken off. People seem to appreciate the extra hours after so much uncertainty."

"It was great," she said, "until it wasn't. I'm assuming you heard about Nick?"

"I did." He sucked the air through his teeth. "I feel for the guy, I really do. It makes me feel terrible about having to fire him two weeks ago."

The detail made Claire sit up and pay attention, all awkwardness temporarily forgotten.

"You fired him?"

"Belinda caught him trying to steal her fundraising money from her locker," he said in a low voice as though someone might overhear them. "Her niece isn't very well, and they're trying to get her to Disneyland. They didn't raise much, so I bumped it up enough to take them to Disneyland Paris. Didn't leave me much choice. It was so out of the blue."

"That's awful," Claire said, almost to herself. "Had he done anything like that before?"

"Model employee until then," he said, taking the turn into the square rather than up to the factory. He stopped outside Claire's shop and pulled on the handbrake. "I've heard stories about his turbulent youth, but between you and me, I think your uncle's influence straightened him out. I overheard a few people say Nick had changed for the worst since Pat went to prison. Pat seemed to take him under his wing."

"How can you do that?"

"Do what?"

"Talk about Pat so easily," she said, the words leaving her mouth before she could wonder if they were a good idea. "He killed your wife."

"Because if I don't," he said, pausing to exhale heavily, "I wouldn't get out of bed in the morning." He yanked his sleeve back, looked at his watch, and said, "I must get to the factory."

Claire hesitated, but the moment was clearly over. Graham ducked and looked into the shop, eyeing up the window display. Claire took the hint, thanked him for the lift, and hurried under the canopy that jutted out from her shop to protect passers-by from weather such as this. Once inside, she smiled, appreciating the novelty of stepping into her very own candle shop, about to open to genuine customers.

"Enjoy it," she said to herself as she flicked the lights on. "You worked hard for this."

Even though she'd arrived early to avoid sitting in the cloud of her parents' tension, a couple of the shops in the square already had their lights on. One of them just happened to be Lilac Gifts. Instead of emerging from her waterproof shell, Claire grabbed a coconut milk candle and bagged it up with a handful of wax melts and a sampler packet of tea lights, each a different summer scent. She'd intended to slowly introduce herself to her fellow shopkeepers over her first week; this venture was merely killing two birds with one stone.

Holding the bag close to her chest, Claire sloshed

across the square, the road underfoot more puddles than cobbles. At Lilac Gifts, Claire was grateful to find the door unlocked. She hurried inside, squinting in the lights that seemed even brighter after the dim storm. She pushed back her hood, and her eyes went straight to the counter. Clearly, she'd interrupted something – the awkwardness in here was as bad as it had been at home and in Graham's car.

Gwyneth was behind the counter, her platinum hair rolled and backcombed to 1950s perfection. She wore a red blouse the same commanding shade as her lips. Gwyneth had drawn one black beauty mark above her top lip and another under her eye, just beneath the sharp point of her expertly drawn wings of eyeliner. A pair of ornate, pink, half-frame glasses connected to a chain of pearls around her neck balanced on the end of her nose. Claire would have guessed Gwyneth was somewhere around the fifty mark, although she looked much younger.

The man on the other side of the counter seemed to be around the same age. His lank, slightly too long combover had thinned to the point where most men would have reached for the clippers. Deep lines were etched in his drawn-out face, and there was a slight sheen to his pastiness. He wore a crinkled brown pinstriped suit, a little too big in all the wrong places and yet still somehow showing an inch of sock above his shoes. A poorly made, bright blue tie looped lazily around an open canary yellow collar. Claire could taste his thick aftershave in the back of her throat; Aramis, she'd know it anywhere.

Some aged like wine, others like cheese.

"I'm not open yet," Gwyneth called across the shop with a smile, her eyes on the clock. "Come back in twenty, honey."

Usually, Claire hated being called 'honey' because it most often came from men trying to belittle her. Gwyneth said it in such a friendly way, it immediately endeared her to Claire.

"My name's Claire Harris," she introduced, holding up the bag. "I've just opened the candle shop across the square. Just wanted to show my face and give you some samples."

"Oh, that's awfully kind of you." Gwyneth smiled and beckoned for Claire to approach as she peered down through her glasses. "I know your face. You're Pat's niece, aren't you?"

Claire cringed internally at the comparison, but she nodded. She was used to being referred to as 'Janet and Alan's daughter,' or even 'DI Harris' daughter.' It had been a while since someone connected her so openly to her uncle. Although she had overheard people talking about 'the situation' and, in turn, Claire's family, people weren't brave enough to be direct about it. Their cutting sideways glances spoke loudly enough. Claire had learned to live with it, but Gwyneth's smile didn't falter. Considering only two days had passed since Nick's death, Gwyneth was holding herself together admirably well.

"I meant to pop over at some point on opening day," Gwyneth said, her smile souring for the first time. "I love candles. Even have my own little range, although I buy them wholesale from the factory."

Claire glanced at the small section in the gift shop, mainly taken up by birthday cards. The simple plain labels said 'Lilac Gifts,' but Claire recognised the products; she'd certainly applied enough of the stickers. While she couldn't compete on price, she was confident the quality of her homemade candles spoke for itself.

"How do you feel opening a direct competitor so close to Gwyn's shop?" asked the man, his voice both scratchier and higher than Claire would have expected. "You could be infringing on her—"

"*Joey!*" Gwyneth silenced the man with a slap on the arm. "There's nothing wrong with a little competition, and besides, I barely sell candles anyway."

Gwyneth leaned in and said to Claire, "Between you and me, you can barely smell them when you light them."

"I promise you won't have the same problem with these," Claire said, offering a genuine smile of her own as she pushed the bag across the counter. "Come over any time. Square discount, of course."

"Same to you," she said, nodding around the shop. "You'll find most shops around the square look out for each other. Except for the chippy, but that's probably for the best. I'd be in there every lunch hour, and I'd never keep my figure!"

Gwyneth laughed, a hand on her unbelievably narrow waist. Claire almost found it cruel that some women could joke about eating fish and chips every day while looking so perfect. Her own waistline was cursed with what Granny Greta called the 'Harris thickness.'

"I'm sorry to hear about Nick," Claire said. "DI Ramsbottom told me you were close."

"That's a breach of your rights!" Joey called. "Uncle or not, he should keep your personal life private."

"Uncle Harry is harmless," she said, rolling her eyes at Joey. "And it's hardly a secret that Nick and I have been running hot and cold for the past twenty years. Give it a rest, will you, Joey?" She turned back to

Claire and softened. "Yes, we were close. I'm devastated, but I can't say I'm surprised."

"You're not?"

"He was always getting himself into trouble," she said, her gaze going to the window and out into the dark square as though in the direction of Nick's house. "He was forever running from someone or something. That's what always drove us apart. I knew something would catch him up eventually, I just never dreamed it would be his own demons."

Gwyneth lifted a shaky hand and rested it against her lips before returning her watery eyes to Claire.

"I really am sorry for your loss." Claire paused to take a deep breath before adding, "I hate to ask now, but do you know if Nick had much contact with Pat since he went to prison?"

"I don't know," Gwyneth said with a shake of her head; her curls didn't move. "Nick didn't like talking about it. Pat was the only role model he had. I think it broke his heart to find out the last good man wasn't good at all." She lifted her index finger to her nose and sniffed back tears. "Is this about Uncle Harry thinking Nick was the one to vandalise the – *Oh*, wait!" She bit into her bottom lip, her eyes widening. "Candle shop. It was *your* shop."

"It was," Claire smiled, almost apologetically. "I was

actually on my way to Nick's to ask him about it when they—"

Claire stopped before she finished the sentence, choosing to let the silence fill in the gaps instead.

"*Alright!*" Joey put an arm across the counter and swept Claire away. "Enough questions." He reached into his pocket and pulled out a card. "You want to talk to Gwyn, you come through me."

"For goodness sake, Joey!" Gwyneth snatched her glasses off and slammed her hands on the counter. "The girl has a right to ask questions. She was connected to Nick through her uncle. You knew Nick as well as I did. I wouldn't have put such dirty tactics past him."

Claire looked down at the card.

Joseph Smith – Lawyer.

"People are looking to point a finger, Gwyn." This time, Joey directed his firmness at Gwyneth. "The ex-girlfriend is the first person they're going to point at. You don't need that right now." He turned to Claire as his eyes darted meaningfully towards the door. "You want to ask questions, you call the number on that card and leave a message with my secretary."

Claire tucked the card away and went to say goodbye to Gwyneth but thought better of it, given Joey's warning. She returned Gwyneth's awkward 'why are men like this?' smile before heading out into the rain that was now coming down even harder. She hurried back to the shop and nearly had a heart attack when Em wandered casually out of the kitchen, blowing into a steaming cup.

"Hope you don't mind," Em said, her clothes soaked through from the rain. "I didn't fancy going to the narrowboat to dry off in this, and I saw your light was on."

"You're always welcome here," Claire said, laughing away her shock. "You know that."

"Thanks, Claire." Em slurped the hot drink before putting it on the counter next to the till. "Nothing like a hot cup of green tea to chase the chill away. I was going to make you a cup of coffee, but I didn't know how to work your machine."

After changing into her dry clothes in the kitchen, Claire turned on her bean-to-cup espresso machine – one of the few luxuries she'd bought when she still worked at the factory and had her own house. It was also one of the few things she kept hold of when she'd moved back to her parents. She'd brought it down, cradled in her arms, before the opening.

The machine whirred to life, crunched up the beans, and poured out a generous cup of black coffee with a rich crema swirling on the surface. After years of weaning herself off the milk and sugar, she'd grown fond enough of the taste of coffee to have it exactly as it came – as long as the beans were good. Coffee was one of the few places she allowed herself to display her mother's snobbish ways.

"Do you know a Joey Smith?" Claire asked, tossing the card onto the counter after fishing it from her pocket. "He basically just threatened to take me to court for trying to talk to Gwyneth."

"Joey?" Em examined the card and chuckled. "Oh, I know him very well. He's always taken himself too seriously." She tossed the card down and picked up her green tea. "Ste, Joey, Gwyn, and I moved in the same circles at school. I was always closest to Ste, but we all got on. Joey and Gwyn were an item back then, but it didn't last long after we left school. Well, not the first time, at least. She met Nick at our twenty-year school reunion. He was sleeping on Ste's couch at the time, so he tagged along even though he was five years younger. I think it was love at first sight for them both, but they were rarely on the same page. Nick couldn't hold it together as much as Gwyn needed him to."

"And Joey stuck around all this time?"

"They don't just call her Marilyn because of her looks," Em said after a sip as sharp as a hiss. "When she wasn't with Nick, she was with Joey. Just when you thought she was about to settle with Nick, he'd do something that sent her back to Joey. When she grew bored with Joey, she went back to Nick." Em set her cup down. "That's the impression I got from Ste, at least. I've been sleeping on his sofa all weekend. Didn't want to leave him. He's torn up."

"Were they close?"

"At times." She bobbed her head from side to side. "Nick's always been very up and down. He would give with one hand, but he'd take with two, and even his brother wasn't immune. From the sounds of it, Nick still owed Ste a considerable amount of money when he died." Em bit her lip and leaned in before adding in a low voice, "Ste is convinced Nick was *murdered*. He just can't wrap his head around his brother doing such a thing."

"I don't think anyone ever can."

"*I* don't see it, Claire," Em insisted, her brows tilting sharply over her eyes. "I knew him his whole life. I'd believe that he sprayed your shop for your uncle, but I can't wrap my head around the idea of him taking his own life. I've searched and searched my soul, but my feelings about this are crystal clear."

Claire pulled her handbag from the plastic bag and retrieved the folded visiting order. She read over the details again though she already had it memorised.

"There's someone else who might know Nick better than anyone," she said, her breath suddenly shaky, handing the card to Em. "It's tomorrow."

"Are you going to visit him?" Em asked without a hint of judgement in her voice.

"Yes," Claire replied firmly, resting a hand on Em's shoulder. "You're the only person I've told. Will you come with me? I don't want to go on my own."

"Of course." Em smiled up at Claire and nodded, patting her hand. "I sense you've got a little time before you need to open. Why don't you go back there and make some candles for fun? Start the day in the right frame of mind, and the rest will slot into place. You can forget about your uncle until we arrive at the prison tomorrow. I'll keep watch here."

Grateful, Claire retreated into the kitchen, and for the first time since developing her range for the shop, gathered her few remaining ingredients, and started playing.

CHAPTER SIX

"The sky is so blue," Claire said, peering through the window of the top deck of the X41 bus as the Manchester cityscape came into view the next afternoon. "Over breakfast, my mum swore we were supposed to get thunder and lightning tonight."

"The calm before the storm." Em wiped beads of sweat from her forehead. "You can feel it in the air."

Claire could. She had opted for what her mother called one of her 'girlie outfits' of thigh-skirting denim shorts and a long, lacey blouse. Even with significantly more skin on show than she usually displayed, the hot air boiled her from the inside. Without the rain to cool things down, the humidity was nearly unbearable. If the bus had air conditioning, it wasn't making a dent.

"I've been coming to Manchester since I was a teenager," Em explained. "Had most of my tattoos done in parlours around the city. The place stayed the same for years, but the gentrification's really taking hold."

Claire had noticed it too, especially over the last decade. The city had sprung upwards, sprouting shiny new office and apartment buildings. Every corner had a chain coffee shop, and the mass of residents thickened with each visit. Her mother had read aloud a magazine article claiming Manchester was 'the new London,' and Claire couldn't disagree. She still loved the place, though. The city had a soul, and its people were much nicer than anything she'd ever experienced in the country's capital.

"It's this next stop," Em said, tapping the visiting order between them, which had been kind enough to include the locations of the nearest transport links. "Let's get downstairs."

They rang a couple of the bells on the way down. The double-decker bus screeched to a halt at a red bus stop, almost throwing them down the narrow staircase to the lower deck. As the doors shuddered open, they thanked the driver and left the bus. Next to the canal as they were, the humidity only worsened. The red-brick tower of the prison loomed above them, not too far away.

"Come on," Em said, nodding down a tight street between two graffiti-covered buildings. "I think I know where it is. I've sailed by here on my narrowboat a few times."

Despite this being her first visit, Claire recognised the front of Her Majesty's Prison Manchester – still more commonly known as its former name, Strangeways – at once. After Strangeways was the scene of an infamous prison riot that brought the country to a standstill in 1990, Claire had been inundated with images of the prison's Victorian entrance of red and beige stone. As famous as the prison was, she'd expected something more imposing. Instead, it existed on a normal-looking city backstreet with old Victorian factories and more modern industrial retail structures surrounding it.

As it turned out, the grand entrance was purely decorative now, with the real access, a less imposing more modern addition, on the corner. Visiting order in hand, Claire and Em joined the steady stream of people walking through the visitor's entrance and forming a queue for the front desk. For the first time in days, she felt the sweet kiss of air conditioning.

"You show the card," Em said as she nodded towards the door the staff were sending visitors through. "Then you go in for your searches. It might seem scary, but you have nothing to hide. Let them do their jobs, and you'll be inside in no time."

Claire nodded shakily, her usually calm composure under attack at the thought of entering prison for the first time. Everything had happened so fast she hadn't given herself a chance to process it.

"Sounds like the voice of experience."

"I have friends all over." Em's smile was stiff. "When you get in there, Claire, just try and remember they're all real people. Real people who have done terrible things, but real people, nonetheless."

"Are my nerves that obvious?" Claire laughed, prompting harsh glares from a few of the guards positioned around the room. "You always know exactly what to say."

"You remind me of myself at your age." Em ducked her head. When she lifted it, her smile had lost its edge. "You're at an age where people start getting stuck in their ways and thinking they have it all figured out. But you, Claire? You're still open to life. The good *and* the bad. *And* you're willing to listen to what people have to say."

"I'm here for my own selfish reasons."

"You say that," Em said softly, bumping their shoulders, "and perhaps it's partly true, but I saw your face when you were reading one of your uncle's letters on the bus. You want to know if it's true." She paused and gave Claire's hand a little squeeze. "Just listen to him. You don't have to believe him. Just listen." She dropped Claire's hand and gave her a little nudge towards the desk. "It's your turn. I can't go any further, but I'll be right here when you get out."

While Em positioned herself cross-legged on one of the plastic chairs attached to the edge of the wall, Claire walked up to the desk.

"Visiting?" barked the uniformed officer behind the desk, tapping away on her screen.

"Pat."

"Pat, *who?*"

"Pat Harris," Claire said, her voice shrinking. "Patrick Harris."

"ID." The woman held her hand out and snapped her fingers. "Come on, love. Haven't got all day, and the queue isn't getting any shorter."

"Right." Claire pulled her purse from her bag and retrieved her pink ID. "It's only a provisional licence. Failed too many times to face another driving test."

The woman's face didn't crack as she checked Claire's face against the ID. She typed something into the screen, slapped the ID on the counter, and slid it back to Claire.

"Don't stand there all day," she demanded. "Door at the end of the hall."

Claire swiped her ID, her heart pounding. She hurried to the door, glancing back at Em one last time before she went in. The subtle thumbs up eased a little of Claire's tension.

As soon as she stepped through the doorway, she was like a calf in a cattle market.

"Phones, shoes, bags in *these* trays," a woman called, holding up two trays to demonstrate like she was at an airport. "When you've filled them, they go over *there* for scanning, and then you go over *here* for your body search."

Claire found a bench and pulled off her sandals; they went in the tray along with her bag and phone. The slightly sticky tiles were the least of her worries. She looked around the search area. At one end was a window into the visiting room. The prisoners were already inside, waiting as approved visitors filtered into a holding room. She imagined Uncle Pat in there, probably as nervous as she was. Em had been right; her stomach fluttered with curiosity about the man she was about to sit and talk with.

After putting her tray on the conveyor belt into a scanner, a guard returned her shoes. Bags weren't allowed inside; she would collect hers at the end.

Stuffing the token the man gave her into her pocket, she joined the line at the full-body scanner.

"No need to be nervous," said a woman about her age. "First time?"

"That obvious?"

"You start to learn the faces," she said with a shrug. "What's yours in for?"

"Oh, erm—"

"Don't be shy, love," she said. "Mine's in for murder. Brother. He won't get out till my kids are our age."

"Murder," Claire replied, liking the woman's forthright tone. "Uncle. He's old enough that I don't think he'll ever get out."

"Considering where they sent him," said the woman as she stepped forwards to take her turn through the scanner, "might be for the best."

Claire waited until they called her. She walked through the scanner, and a woman with blue gloves beckoned her over. The guard checked Claire's waistband, hair, and mouth before she was satisfied and waved towards the holding group. Most visitors were already looking through the window; a few even waved and tried to communicate silently through it. Although a handful of the visitors were men, most were women. The mothers, sisters, daughters of people like Pat.

For the first time since her uncle's arrest, Claire didn't feel quite so alone.

Head down, Claire waited until the door finally clicked open. One by one, everyone filed into the large room. She didn't look up until she crossed over into the stuffy visiting area. Men in red bibs waited behind single desks in the sterile room. Some looked like the stereotypical 'violent criminal' of news and TV with facial tattoos and broken noses. Still, most looked like any man she'd pass on the street and not look twice at. There were people of all ages, from men who barely looked old enough to drink, to men so old they looked like they had already spent their lifetimes inside. Remembering Em's advice about them being real people, she inhaled deeply as she looked for Uncle Pat.

By the time she spotted him in the back corner, he was already staring at her. He greeted her with a raised hand, but she couldn't bring herself to return it. She wasn't sure if she'd been expecting arched eyebrows and devil horns, but he still looked like she remembered, if a little thinner. Eyes on the tiles, she made her way to the chair and sat down.

"Claire, I—"

"*Don't*," she said, a faint whiff of hysteria in the back of her voice. "Don't say anything." She clenched her eyes and looked up at the ceiling, tears clouding her vision. "How could you do this to us? You've broken our family."

"Claire, I know, I—"

"I said, *don't*." Her voice came out louder than she expected, prompting a few shushes from the watching guards. "I'm sorry. I wasn't sure how I would react to seeing you. Now I know."

"I've seen worse," he replied, his smile familiar and strangely comforting. "Thanks for coming. I've missed you."

Claire wiped her tears and rolled her eyes, still unable to make sustained eye contact. He looked too much like her father, and visiting him was as close to betraying him as she'd ever got.

"I thought I might see you at the trial," he said after a period of silence.

"We stayed as far away as we could," she said, roughly dashing away more tears with the back of her hand as she caught her breath. "Not that it mattered. It was still plastered all over the front page of the *Northash Observer* for everyone to see. Mum ran around the village trying to buy up every copy, but there's no putting what you did back in a box. We have to live with it. I have to look Graham in the eye almost every day knowing what you did – actually, *no* – he has to look *me* in the eye knowing *my* uncle murdered his wife."

Claire stopped talking; her volume was rising again. She took a calming breath and remembered Em's advice about listening. She clasped her hands together and looked at Pat; his expression echoed the horror she felt.

"I know," he said, his bottom lip wobbling. "I know what I did. I killed two people. I live with that every day. I know I get it easy being in here, and I'm sorry for that. I really am, Claire. But I can't change what I did. It's done." He paused and looked down at his own clasped hands. "I've had a lot of time to reflect. I was so angry about Nicola's indifference to Bilal's death. I wasn't thinking straight. She was just so dismissive! She didn't care that her lax safety checks allowed him to fall into that vat of wax at the factory. And I had to see his father, Abdul, day in day out, hurting from what she did." He frowned and inhaled on a pained hiss. "That being said, she didn't deserve to die. Neither did Jeff. I know I deserve to be here. I just hoped my family would come and see me. I have no one, Claire. No one."

"You did it to yourself." The tears she wiped away now were ones of anger. "Well, your little plan worked. I got the hint. I'm here."

"I didn't know what to do," he said in a low,

pleading voice. "I thought if I kept sending letters, I'd—"

"I'm not talking about the *letters!*" she cried. Another chorus of shushing followed. "I'm talking about the spray paint. *Congratulations?* Hardly subtle."

"W-wha – Claire, I – Congratulations?"

"The paint," she repeated, forcing her tone to flatten. "All over the front of my shop the day before opening. I know it was you. I followed the breadcrumbs back to Nick."

"What paint?" he asked, shaking his head. "What *shop*? What opening?"

"*My* shop," she said. "My candle shop."

"You finally opened your dream candle shop?" He lifted his hand up to his face. "Claire, I-I'm so proud of you."

Claire stared open-mouthed at her uncle, unsure if she should laugh or cry. Just when she was wondering if she should believe him, she remembered how easily he'd lied about murder right up until he couldn't hide it anymore. Em's advice about not having to believe him pushed to the forefront of her mind. When she closed her eyes, she saw Nick's lifeless body as if she were standing in front of it all over again.

"Someone vandalised my shop," she said, slowly and carefully. "Ryan showed me video footage of Nick with spray paint, and then we went to his house and found him dead."

"*What?*" Pat cried, earning a few shushes of his own. "Nick's *dead?*"

"No one told you?"

"Claire, I meant it when I said I have no one." Tears lined his eyes, and he frowned at the floor as they fell. "How-how did he die?"

"He hanged himself."

"No, he can't have." Pat's eyes clenched shut. "He wouldn't. He couldn't. I knew him better than anyone. His mother committed suicide when he was a teenager. It sent him off the rails. It *broke* him. He insisted he'd never do that to people – to his brother – no matter how desperate things were. He understood too deeply how that kind of loss rippled through the lives of those left behind. Nick wouldn't have taken his life. It wasn't in his character."

"How well do we ever know anyone?" Claire asked, her gaze fixed firmly on her uncle. "I-I think this was a mistake."

Claire went to pull away from the table, to leave, but Pat dove across and grabbed her hands. One of the guards swooped in and pulled him back, sternly reminding him about the no touching rule. Claire motioned that she was okay and resettled into the seat, albeit at a slight angle towards the exit, ready to move at a moment's notice.

"Ste thinks his brother was murdered," she said, chewing the inside of her cheek. "Would you know anything about *that*?"

"Are you suggesting *I* had Nick killed from the inside?" Pat laughed away the suggestion. "Claire, I'm still *me*. I made a lot of mistakes in the heat of the moment, but I'm the same person I always was."

"No." She shook her head. "You're not. Because the uncle I thought I knew would never have resorted to murder."

"We all have it in us," he said, eyelashes trembling above his unblinking gaze. "The darkness. In a moment of weakness, I let the monster in. We can all pretend it's not there, but it is. Every one of us is a single decision away from ruining our lives at every moment. I just – I wish I hadn't taken yours – the family's – down with mine. I knew it would be awful for you, but I didn't realise how bad."

"Aren't you going to ask about him?"

"Your father, I presume?" He smiled sourly down at the desk. "I don't need to. I know what this did to him. What *I* did to him, my big brother. I haven't been able to bring myself to write to him, but I—"

"Don't."

"Claire, I—"

"And stop writing to me too." She stood, attracting the attention of those around her. "You did this to yourself, Pat. Nobody held your hand when you pushed Nicola to her death. Deal with it, just like we are."

He nodded as though he understood. "Will you visit again?"

Claire couldn't think of an answer, so she said nothing as she stared down at him, unable to sit but also unable to leave.

"It was nice seeing you," he said, eyes back on the table, "you might want to ask your gran about the casino. It's the only thing I can think of that might have got Nick into trouble."

"What casino?"

"Just ask her," he said, his tone withdrawn. "Thanks for coming."

Claire didn't linger in her uncle's sorrow. She made her way back to the waiting area and the comfort of the air conditioning. After another quick search, she traded in the token for her bag. Back in the reception area, Em was comforting a sobbing elderly woman. Not wanting to interrupt, Claire headed straight outside. Eyes closed, she leaned her head against the red brick and turned her face to the sky. The air was as stuffy as ever, but she managed her first full breath since entering the prison.

"Poor thing's first time visiting her son," Em explained to Claire when she joined her against the wall. "How did it go?"

Claire opened her eyes and letting out her exhale. "It happened. And I was there. I'll process it later."

"The first visit is always the hardest."

"Who says I'm coming back?"

"You will." Em wrapped her hand around Claire's and tugged her in the opposite direction of the bus stop. "I already used the payphone inside to call Sally, and she's happy to watch the shop. I told her you were having a filling at the dentist, so maybe clutch your cheek when you go back."

"Thank you."

"Come on," Em suggested, linking arms with Claire as they set off in the shadow of the tall prison walls. "It would be rude to come all this way and not have a drink. I know a place."

CHAPTER SEVEN

"The X41 should be here soon," Em said as she gulped down the last of the water she'd ordered. "Let's make a move."

Claire slurped to the bottom of her raspberry vodka and lemonade. After the surreal prison visit, she couldn't have ordered anything weaker than vodka; it took a stiff drink to bring her back down. Besides, the party had already started in the pub. It would have been rude to order something straightforward as a pint of lager, and she'd never seen raspberry vodka before.

"You'd never think it was the middle of the afternoon," Claire called over the music as she slid off the high stool next to a flashing gambling machine.

"It's a shame I have a shop to get back to. Getting day drunk right now seems appropriate."

"That's Canal Street for you," Em said with a chuckle, directing Claire to the door. "The stop's just around the corner."

The sun blinded Claire as she walked out of the dark disco lights and into the bright afternoon. The crystal-blue sky made a mockery of the storm warning, but the sticky air had only thickened. Barely clothed people wearing sunglasses filled the outdoor tables between the row of pubs and bars and the canal, squeezing in the only chance they'd had to sunbathe all week.

"Almost feels a shame to rush off," Claire said as she followed Em down a back street under a canopy of rainbow bunting. "Who knows how long it'll be until we get another dry patch."

"All storms end," Em mused as they turned into a dark, cobbled alley between two tall rows of pubs. "Even the terrible ones."

Claire stayed right on Em's heels as she took more twists and turns around corner after corner. Em seemed to know the city streets like the back of her hand, only emphasising how poorly Claire knew it despite countless visits over the years. She didn't recognise anything until they reached a red bus stop across from a multi-story carpark; she'd waited there with Sally after enough shopping trips as teenagers to find it familiar.

"I think that's ours," Em said, picking up the pace as the bus door shuddered shut. "Wait for us!"

Side by side, they ran down the long street towards the bus. They reached the red stop just as the double-decker pulled away from the kerb. The unsmiling faces of the passengers stared down at them, and not one called for the driver to stop. Hands in her short hair, Claire watched the bus drive away and turn past the large carpark.

"I don't suppose the buses are more regular these days?" Claire asked as she attempted to study the timetable. "They were a nightmare when I was a kid. I can't tell you how many times Sally and I lingered here for hours."

"Oh, they're more regular," Em said, tracing her finger along the X41 line. "Just not the ones going through Northash." She stabbed her finger on the plastic. "Looks like it's going to be a two-hour wait until the next. We could catch the X40 as far as Clitheroe and hire a taxi from there?"

"I'm feeling rich at the moment thanks to the success of opening morning." Claire pulled her phone from her pocket and opened the new Northash Taxi app a recent flyer had instructed her to download. A couple of taps later, she said, "Done. Says it will be here in forty minutes. I'm sure we can kill time until then."

"There is no killing time," Em said, looping her arm through Claire's and setting off down the road, "only life to live. C'mon, I know another place."

The place turned out to be Afflecks, a four-storey Victorian shopping emporium dedicated to the weird and wonderful. Against a backdrop of walls covered in art and graffiti (much nicer than the stuff her shop had experienced), they wandered from small vintage clothes shops to record shops to shops filled with crystals. There were also a significant number of places to get piercings and tattoos, as well as plenty of eateries. Em seemed to know everyone, and everyone seemed to know Em – especially the tattoo artists. Three separate shop owners waved Em in to check up on their work on her fully inked body, and Em introduced Claire to them all. By the time the app notified her of the driver's close proximity, Claire had bought six different candles from three different boutique shops and a few bath bombs. They'd even had a cup of tea in a café on the top floor.

Bag of goodies in hand, Claire followed Em back to the red bus stop with lifted spirits; being in Em's company tended to do that. When the Northash Taxi car rolled around the corner, and she saw the driver, the reason she'd needed her spirits lifting in the first place slammed home.

"Isn't it a bit soon?" Claire asked as Ste pulled up next to them on the kerb.

"This is just Ste's way," Em said, waving to her old friend. "He always keeps going."

Em took the front seat, leaving Claire to climb into the back. Ste, a large, bald man in a baggy polo shirt, smiled and nodded his recognition in the rear-view mirror. Claire returned the smile. He immediately looked away, and, too late, she realised her lips had formed the same tight, sympathetic smile she'd so hated seeing after her uncle's arrest. Ste set off before either of them had a chance to fasten their seatbelts.

"Ramsbottom rang me on my drive over," he said flatly, leaning across the steering wheel to look up and down either side of a busy city junction. "I knew it wasn't suicide, Em. I told you it wouldn't be. Not after our mum. He wouldn't." Ste indicated left, and then immediately changed his mind and shot across the road, indicating right before squeezing into a full line of traffic – the bus he cut off blared its horn. "What're those people called who look at bodies to figure it out?"

"Pathologists," Em replied.

"That's them." He glanced in the rear-view mirror at the traffic behind Claire before relaxing into the jam he'd just crammed them into. "Ramsbottom said something about the rope marks on his neck not being consistent with hanging. He wouldn't say what they were consistent with, but it doesn't take a genius to figure it out, does it? Someone's gone and strangled the poor fella."

The humid city rushed noisily around them as they crawled forward, but in the close confines of the taxi, Claire could have heard a pin drop. The revelation hung uncomfortably in the air as they all wrestled with the idea of anyone using suicide to frame a murder. Em reached across the gear stick and rested her hand on Ste's. He clenched the steering wheel and sniffled as if crying; Claire didn't look in the mirror to confirm it.

"He wasn't perfect. I know it better than anyone," Ste said as he turned at the next corner, breaking free of one stream of traffic only to tack onto the back of another. "I tried my best in raising him, but I was only a teenager myself when Mum died. It was hard keeping him out of trouble. Every time I thought he was on the straight and narrow, he'd come running to me for help. It was always about money, and I always tried to help. I should have known he was in trouble when he came begging for twelve grand."

"Twelve thousand pounds?" Em echoed the sum. "Ste, you never said it was that much."

"I could only get him five," he replied with a sigh. "He promised I'd have it back immediately, but that was his usual line. I wasn't expecting it back overnight, but I suppose it's as good as gone now."

"What would he need that kind of money for?" Em asked.

"Knowing my brother," Ste said, finally turning into a clear road, "I'd say gambling debts."

Claire barely knew Ste and hesitated a moment before giving in to the temptation.

"Speaking of gambling," asked Claire, edging forward in the middle seat to join the conversation. "Do you know if Nick frequented any casinos?"

"Casinos?" Ste grunted a laugh. "Nick? Not unless you call the local bookies a casino, no. Dogs or horses, it didn't matter to him. Betting on the races kept the man skint for most of his life." He glanced at her in the rear-view. "Why'd you ask?"

"Something my uncle said."

"You've just gone to see Pat?" Ste let out another forced laugh with a slight headshake. "Still can't believe what he did, but that's life, isn't it? As much as we want people to be good, it means nothing when the chips are down. How's prison treating him?"

"As you'd expect," was all she could manage. "Did Nick ever visit him?"

"Never mentioned it."

They left the city and eventually merged onto the M66 motorway back to Northash. They remained in silence until the taxi pulled up in the village square directly outside Claire's Candles.

"I don't know if it would be considered a casino," Ste said, yanking the handbrake before turning as much as he could in his seat, "but I just had a thought. Around the time your uncle went to prison, Nick asked me to join a card ring he'd set up. Wanted me to invest in it – typical Nick, cheeky enough to ask. I keep on the straight and narrow, but I went along just the once." He looked around as if fearing someone might be listening in. "It was all pretty low stakes. A couple of quid here and there. I was surprised by the number of people."

"Who?" Claire asked, on the edge of her seat.

"Gwyneth," he said, nodding at Lilac Gifts. "They were together at the time, I think. Malcolm and Theresa from the pub, Eugene from the café. Agnes and Jeanie from the B&B were there too. Couple of faces I couldn't put names to, but the cellar was pretty packed out."

"Don't tell me." Claire inhaled deeply and exhaled in a rush. "My uncle's cellar?"

Ste nodded.

"Thank you," she said, opening the app to pay the fare. "You've just saved me an awkward conversation with my gran."

"She's the little woman with the dog, isn't she?" Ste asked, back to looking at Claire in the mirror again. "She was there too."

"My gran?" Her stomach flipped. "Part of an underground gambling ring?" She paused to put her phone back. "Saying that, she does put the lottery on four times a week without fail."

"Explains why your uncle told you to ask her," Em said as she unclipped her seatbelt. She leaned over to kiss Ste on the cheek. "Thanks for getting us back so quickly. I'll pop 'round later."

Claire waited until Ste's car rounded the corner before turning to look at her shop. Three customers browsed inside, and Sally seemed to be handling it with ease – not that Claire doubted she could. Maybe Sally wasn't the best timekeeper, but she juggled more than anyone else Claire knew and made it look somewhat easy.

"Even the stains scrubbed hardest leave shadows," said Em, reaching out to scratch a little remaining red paint from one of the small windowpanes. "I assume your uncle didn't confess to putting Nick up to the vandalization?"

"He went one step further," Claire replied, biting the inside of her cheek. "Made out like he had no idea the shop even existed. His denial was pretty convincing, but it's not like he has a problem with lying. I don't know what to believe."

"Listen to your heart," Em said, giving Claire a hug. "Which is what I'm going to do. I need to help Ste figure this out. He might put up a brave front, but he'll be a wreck on the inside until his brother has some peace."

"Do you think it could be connected to the cellar card club?" Claire asked, looking in the direction of Lilac Gifts.

"It's as good a place to start as any," Em said, already stepping back into the road. "I'll talk to Gwyn. She won't lie to me. If anyone knows what Nick was up to in his final days, it'll be her."

"Hopefully, you don't have to go through the lawyer."

"Joey Smith doesn't scare me," she said with a laugh and a wave. "Keep your ear to the ground."

As Em began her walk across the square, Claire hesitated at her shop door. She needed to keep more than an ear to the ground. She might not have declared her intention to solve the mystery aloud like Em, but she couldn't stop her mind scratching for a solution, especially now that DI Ramsbottom had officially opened a murder investigation. Once again, she was too connected to the case to look the other way.

For now, at least, she had a shop to close. As soon as she stepped inside, the sea of scents immediately brought a smile to her face. Sally was behind the counter serving a young woman with a full basket; her two daughters, Ellie and Aria, sprawled on the floor at her feet with their faces buried in computer tablets.

"Sorry I'm so late," she said after the customer left. Sally kissed her on each cheek. "We missed the bus and then had to wait for a taxi."

"Don't apologise! Compared to running around Lancashire showing posh people posh houses, this was a treat. Nice to stand in one place." Sally peered into the bag of candles Claire had bought. "And here I was thinking you had enough."

She laughed. "It'll never be enough."

"How's your tooth?"

Claire clutched her cheek, remembering the alibi

Em had given over the phone. She immediately dropped it, glancing at the kids over Sally's shoulder.

"What is it?" Sally whispered, leaning in closer. "Don't mind them. I could scream their names at top volume and they wouldn't look up from those things."

Claire waited until the last customer left and immediately flipped the sign to CLOSED. Once alone, she pulled Sally into the kitchen, out of the kids' earshot.

"I went to visit my uncle."

"I *knew* it!" Sally slapped her on the arm. "Em can't lie in the slightest. She's too nice." She bit her lip and rested the same hand in the same spot, gently this time. "How are you feeling, mate?"

"I'll tell you when I figure it out." Claire leaned in. "Estate agents keep copies of keys, don't they?"

"When we manage the property on behalf of landlords," she said, folding her arms. "This is going where I think it is, isn't it?"

Claire and Sally had been able to read each other's minds since childhood. She scrunched up her face and nodded.

"It's a good job you're probably the only person I trust lately," Sally said, grabbing her handbag off the hooks on the wall. She plucked a set of keys from her bag and held them up. "I need a favour in return."

"Anything."

"I think you'll regret saying that," Sally said, still holding up the keys. "The property needs to be empty before people can view it. We also need to give the family a chance to recover anything they'd like to save. Your gran's listed as Pat's next of kin, but I'm not about to ask a woman in her eighties to sift through her son's bedroom before the removal people come to clear it out."

"Toss it all," Claire replied flatly.

"Your choice." Sally threw her the keys. "You might as well have a look though, mate."

CHAPTER EIGHT

After locking up the shop, Claire went straight to her gran's cottage. She knocked and waited for a few moments, but no answer came. Greta didn't have a mobile phone, but she did have an active social life and the list of places she could be was a long one. Claire wasn't in the mood to search the whole village for her.

She also wasn't in the mood to go home and look her father in the eye without telling him where she'd spent a good chunk of her afternoon. After the awkwardness of breakfast, she imagined dinner could only be worse. She sent her mother a text message fibbing about having a girls' night with Sally before heading to The Park Inn.

Though The Park Inn was the more attractive of Northash's two pubs, it couldn't compete with The Hesketh Arms on much else. Even ignoring the better food, award-winning locally famous homebrew, and lower prices at Hesketh, a chain pub like The Park Inn just couldn't replicate the homey welcome Theresa and Malcolm so effortlessly created. Some joked The Park Inn was the pub people in the village went to have affairs since so few locals ever darkened its doorway. Others called it a decoy pub, leaving the Hesketh for locals to enjoy – the best-kept secret in the village.

Alone in the corner, Claire sampled the cheese and onion pie off the new menu. One rubbery bite was all she needed – obviously, it was fresh from a microwave. Claire Harris: the one fool in Northash gullible enough to pay £8.99 for a meal based on a rumour of 'the new menu not being so bad, apparently.' She'd happily report her findings to Theresa and Malcolm the next time she was in her true local.

Of course, Claire wasn't in The Park Inn to sample the microwave pie and chunky chips still slightly frozen in the middle.

She scanned the room for faces she recognised but none jumped out. Tonight, a room full of strangers suited Claire fine. She'd rather not risk being exposed by the ever-observant eyes and ears of Northash as she hid out until the sun wasn't quite so high in the sky.

The sky blackened before Claire could decide if she wanted to risk the dessert menu. She glanced at the clock, but it was still hours before sunset. A deep, distant rumble of thunder echoed around the pub, silencing the few strangers. Claire stood, finishing her pint with one hand while reaching for her denim jacket with the other. She wasn't alone. One by one, people settled their bills and headed for the door. The people passing through Northash were probably keen to get home, but Claire had somewhere else to be. She tucked a shiny, red ten-pound note under her plate and left.

A whistling wind whipped her short hair into her eyes as she hurried down the steep road towards the square. Pausing outside the closed post office on the corner, she glanced up at Starfall Park. Ominous, velvety black clouds had already advanced beyond the observatory at the top of the steep incline.

Taking advantage of the absence of rain, Claire sped up until she was very nearly at a jog. She turned left at the butchers on the corner and headed towards Christ Church Square, but skidded to a stop on the corner of Warton Lane across from the church when she saw Damon and Ryan deep in conversation a little further up the narrow pavement. Damon was in his factory-issued lumpy blue jumpsuit, and Ryan in his usual gym wear, chunky white headphones around his neck. Under the natural rooftop created by the lush leaves of the trees on either side of the road, known locally as The Canopies, the sudden change in weather wasn't noticeable.

"Not really the right time for a casual chat outside," Claire called up the road as she hurried towards them. "What are you two doing up here?"

"Just catching up," Ryan said, grinning down at Claire. "You been running, mate? You're as red as a beetroot."

Claire hadn't noticed Ryan and Damon talking much since Ryan's return. They'd all gone to the same high school, but they'd moved in different friend groups. Claire and Sally stuck together like Velcro, Ryan had his art friends, and Damon hid away in the library.

"Storm's coming." She hooked her thumb over her shoulder in the direction of the park. "Didn't you hear the thunder?"

"What thunder?" Damon pushed up his glasses as he squinted up at the dense trees. "Although, now that you mention it, it's a little dark. Usually still bright when I walk home from work this time of year."

"And when I go for my after work run," Ryan added, his gaze echoing Damon's.

"You go running after work?" Claire asked, arching a brow. "You work in a *gym*."

"Old habits die hard," he said, wiping the humid shine from his freckled, flushed cheeks. "I miss running on a beach, but the English countryside is the next best thing."

"Yeah?" Claire flinched as another rumble of thunder boomed up the narrow lane. "That countryside's about to be washed away any second. Fancy coming with me to check out my uncle's cottage? It's only around the corner."

Purple lightning lit the sky even through the canopy of leaves, and the thunder followed seconds behind. Warm rain fell in a heavy sheet, like someone had just twisted a shower knob to full pressure. Claire didn't wait around for an answer. She sprinted towards her destination faster than she'd done since the days of P.E. and forced runs up Killer Hill.

Guided by desperation and familiarity, she ran at the cottage's front door with the key outstretched. It slotted into the lock. She twisted it and fell into the dark cottage without resistance. Ryan sprinted in right behind her, with Damon bringing up the rear seconds later.

"*Woo!*" Ryan let out a cheer as he shook rain from his red hair. "Doesn't that just make you feel alive?"

"Sure. Alive." Damon slammed the door and leaned against it before pulling off his wonky glasses. "Just the word I'd use."

While Claire and Damon caught their breath, the three of them lingered in the dark hall, eyes fixed on the textured ceiling. Outside, the downpour somehow intensified. Lightning lit up the hallway, and the nearly simultaneous thunder was loud enough to make them all jump. Sturdy as the cottages in Northash seemed, Claire wouldn't have been surprised if the entire top floor of the house had ripped off just then.

"Looks like we're waiting it out in here for a while," Claire said, testing the light switch several times to no avail. "Good job it's warm, I guess."

"I'll go look for towels," Ryan said, removing his headphones before peeling off the soaked vest that he then balled up and threw on the floor by the door.

"And I'll go and look for something to drink," Damon said, waiting until Ryan had sprinted up the stairs to unzip his blue jumpsuit and reveal his equally soaked undershirt. "It's enough to make you sick, isn't it? Just think, if we'd kept up with the gym like he did, *we* could look like that by now."

"We went three times twelve years ago," Claire reminded him, leaning her head against his shoulder as they entered the dark kitchen. "I like you just as you are, Damon Gilbert."

"But if I looked like *that*," he said, nodding up at the ceiling, "I'd have the women on the dating apps liking me too."

Claire's gaze followed Damon's but she had to glance away again when the beams in the ceiling reminded her of what she'd seen from the square the afternoon of Nick's murder. Though she'd looked away before she could absorb any of the details, she had a feeling they were directly where he'd been.

"You're back on the apps?" she asked, hurrying out of the hallway and heading straight to the fridge. "I thought you'd sworn off them?" She opened the door, and even though the light didn't turn on, she spotted three four-packs of beer. "Jackpot."

Claire reached for one of the four-packs, pulled out a can, and tossed it to Damon. Without complaining about the beer being warm or cheap, he cracked it open immediately.

"Just having a look at who's out there these days." He took a long pull of his beer. "It's a small dating pool 'round here. Starting to think my mum's right. Maybe being alone isn't all it's cracked up to be."

"You're not alone, Damon."

"I know," he replied, blushing. "I didn't mean it like that. It's just . . . I'm thirty-six next month, and I can't help but feel I should have a family or something by this point. Instead, I'm planning to meet up with my internet mates again for a convention."

"Do you like them?"

"They're my best friends," he said before quickly adding, "besides you."

"Then that sounds like a birthday well spent." Claire opened her beer and tapped the rim to Damon's. "Em would say something like 'love comes in all forms,' or 'don't sit around waiting to be happy,' and she'd be right. Live in the moment." Sipping the warm beer took her right back to her teen years and sneaking drinks with Ryan when their mothers were looking the other way. "It'll all slot into place when you least expect it, I'm sure."

Ryan bombed down the stairs with three towels and a handful of large, dry t-shirts. Neither asked if he'd pulled them from the murderer's or the dead man's room, but they changed into them all the same. In separate rooms, on Damon's request.

"So," Ryan asked as he reached for one of the

unopened cans of beer, "you here to find the spray paint?"

"I hadn't thought of that," she said, looking around. "I suppose it could be here if he didn't throw it away immediately. But no, that's not why I came." She looked up at the cursed beam in the ceiling and gulped. "I went to see my uncle today, and before either of you ask, no, I don't know how I feel about it yet." She paused to swallow another mouthful of beer before adding, "Long story short, my uncle mentioned something about a casino, and Nick's brother confirmed that some kind of card ring was being run in the cellar."

"You think it might be connected to Nick's death?" Damon asked, voice slightly muffled as he towelled off his dark hair.

"My uncle thought it was important enough to mention." She looked around the dark kitchen as another flash of lightning momentarily lit up the shadows. "That, or he's playing more games with me."

"Then what are we waiting for?" Ryan took a big gulp of his drink before slamming his can of beer down on the kitchen counter. "Where's the cellar?"

"I'm not too sure," she admitted, scanning the doors in the kitchen. "My uncle had lodgers for as long as I can remember. It was something of an unspoken rule that we didn't turn up at his house all that often. Nick had to have been here for at least a decade, and we really never got to know him." Her stare blurred out of focus as she gazed at the kitchen tiles. "I suppose there's a lot about my uncle's life that I didn't really know."

"Mate," Damon called, nodding for Claire to join him in the shadowy corner where he was shining his phone. "Think I found the door to the cellar."

"How do you know?"

Damon shone his light over a shiny gold plaque mounted in the middle of the door. 'Pat's Casino' was engraved in large, bold letters. Claire smiled and, for a moment, forgot about her uncle as the murderer and remembered him instead as the man with a dry sense of humour who gave his all to everything.

"Hardly a big secret," she said, pulling open the door. "After you?"

"Nah, I'm alright." Damon looked down the dark staircase as more lightning briefly illuminated the kitchen. "I only came because it was closer than my house – and how many times can you say you've visited the house of a murderer? No offence. But I am not walking down into a haunted cellar. I've seen enough films to know how that pans out."

Claire was about to laugh off the suggestion that

the cellar was haunted, but the storm outside offered its brightest, loudest performance right on cue.

"Why don't we go down and find out," Ryan said, lighting a jar candle with a box of matches from the sideboard. He lifted it up to his face, and with a creepy, shadowy grin said, "Or are you too *scaaaared*?"

"Very funny." Claire whacked him with the back of her hand – thunder punctuated the contact. "I vote you go first. You have the biggest muscles."

"I second that," Damon said, edging behind Claire. "Although I'm not sure what good muscles would do against a ghost. Theoretically. We'd be much better off with a proton pack, like the ones from *Ghostbusters*. Yes, they're technically fictional and they—"

"And just like that I'm not scared," Claire announced, taking the candle from Ryan. "Thanks, Damon. I ain't afraid of no ghost!"

Taking the steps quickly and firmly, Claire descended the smooth stone staircase into the darkness, guided only by the faint, flickering light of the candle. At the bottom, she reached a wooden door with another plaque: 'Members Only Beyond This Point.' Claire hadn't considered that her uncle would have been the founder of the 'casino.' It was impossible not to imagine him having a chuckle as he put up the signs; so far, the level of detail had 'Pat' written all over it.

Fingers wrapped around the cold doorknob, she twisted and pushed inwards, the candle guiding the way. The soft glow lit up the compact room, which looked far more professional than the simple round table and deck chairs she'd pictured based on Ste's 'card ring' comments.

"You're kidding me," Ryan said as he followed her in. "Why are we suddenly in Las Vegas?"

Claire set the candle down in the middle of a table with cards from the last-played game still strewn about the surface. Once the flame settled, it illuminated a giant sign on the wall that, indeed, said, 'Welcome to Las Vegas.' A large, framed picture of two men posing in front of a mega-casino filled the opposite wall. The height difference between Pat, a short man like Claire's father, and Nick, a giant by anyone's standards, was almost comical. From the beaming grin on Nick's face, she imagined Pat would be smiling too; someone had scratched his face out.

"He talked about that Vegas holiday for years," Claire said, drinking in every detail of her uncle's passion project. "Every year he'd swear he was going to go back, 'only when the money is right.'"

"I guess this was one way to make that money,"

Ryan said, grabbing the candle and taking it over to a roulette wheel in the corner. "This thing is covered in receipts. I think they're from the bookies 'round the corner from the gym."

Claire joined him in the corner and peered at the dozens of scrunched up betting slips.

"They're all dated the day before Nick died," Ryan said quietly as he uncrumpled a few. "Some for hundreds. This one for almost a thousand. Lost on most of them by the looks of it."

"What's going on down there?" Damon cried. "You've gone quiet."

"Ghost killed us," Claire called back. "Come down. We need your brain."

Damon took the stairs at lightning speed, his thudding footsteps standing in place of the rumbling thunder they couldn't hear below ground level.

"Add all these up," Claire said. "I bet it's around five thousand."

Damon, ever the human calculator, only needed to scan each ticket briefly before moving to the next, his calm face showing no indication that he was doing mental arithmetic. Claire had never understood how easily her friend could add, subtract, and divide at will – especially without using his fingers and having his tongue sticking out as she'd have done in his place.

"He spent £7553," he said after dropping the last slip, "but I kept a running total of the winnings and, assuming he re-invested every penny he won over what was a long day betting on horses and dogs, his original spending money would come to £4987."

"Close enough."

"How did you know that?" Ryan asked.

"Nick's brother, Ste, said he gave him five thousand pounds not long before his brother died," she revealed, picking up the candle and holding it up to the hollow of her uncle's missing face. "Ste also said that Nick asked to borrow twelve thousand pounds."

"Oddly specific," Damon pointed out, "almost like he owed someone twelve thousand pounds and was trying to make up the difference on the races."

"But he lost every penny of it?" Ryan fluttered his lips with a heavy breath. "No wonder the poor fella killed hims—"

"He didn't," Claire cut in, realising the news hadn't reached every corner of the village yet. "Ramsbottom has opened a murder case. Rope marks inconsistent with hanging. A debt of twelve thousand pounds is as good a motive as any."

"And I've found you a list of suspects," Damon called from a small side table. "There's a guestbook here, and there are four names listed as attending the last meeting."

"Please tell me my gran isn't on there."

"No." Damon glanced over his shoulder, nodded at Ryan, and said, "but your landlord is. Agnes, Gwyn, Joey, and Nick. It's dated the day before he died."

"Agnes?" Ryan laughed. "Didn't have her down as the gambling type. Might be worth talking to her to see what she knows?"

Claire nodded, her gaze homing in on the candle as the overwhelmingly familiar scent filled the small room. While she'd been passionately developing what she referred to as 'the best vanilla candle formula of all time' earlier in the year, she'd given this prototype to her uncle. He'd always offered the best advice, had always been as focused on her dream of opening a candle shop as she was. Thinking back, he might have been the first person to whom she revealed that dream – probably over a pint of Hesketh Homebrew at the pub.

"C'mon," she said, picking up the candle. "Let's go and wait for this storm to pass. There's probably some biscuits or crisps in the—"

Claire's stopped abruptly, and all of them whipped around to look up at the low, exposed-beam ceiling. Fast footsteps banged across the creaky wood.

"I knew this was a bad idea," Damon whined, turning straight to the stairs. "I'm going to take my chances out in the—"

Damon let out a high-pitched scream as electric purple lightning split the sky in two. The silhouette of a hunched figured hissed from the top of the stairs, its hair and tail standing on end.

CHAPTER NINE

"*Pickles?*" Claire called up the stairs, pushing past a trembling Damon. "I forgot my uncle had a cat."

"C-cat?" Damon cried, scrambling up the stairs on her heels. "It sounded like Usain Bolt himself sprinted across that floor."

"He's a big cat."

Pickles, a large ginger shorthair, backed away from Claire. His head recoiled as he hissed again, his eyes as wide as saucers. How many days had it been since his last meal? Rather than trying to appease the cat with words or affection, Claire searched the cupboards. She came across two tins of tuna first. She popped the lids off, and Pickles launched onto the counter to bury his face in one before she had a chance to dump them into a bowl.

"Poor thing must be starving," she said, filling a dish with water. "Must be days since he's eaten properly." She set the water on the floor and dumped the second tin of tuna onto a saucer. After searching more cupboards, she found a box of biscuits and poured as many as would fit into another bowl. "Poor guy's been forgotten about."

Leaving Pickles to fill his boots, they went through to the sitting room at the front of the cottage with the rest of the beer. In contrast to the highly polished cellar, the rest of the house was decorated as simply as could be: white walls, a grey sofa with a matching armchair, a coffee table, and a small television on a stand in the corner. With no rugs, cushions, pictures, or even a mirror, it definitely missed what her mother would call 'a woman's touch.'

"Shame the power isn't on," Damon said, squatting to scan the DVDs on the shelf under the TV. "There's some *Doctor Who* boxsets here. Didn't know your uncle was a Whovian."

"A what?" Ryan laughed, dropping onto the left side of the sofa in a sprawl.

"It's a name for people who like *Doctor Who*,"

Damon said in a quieter voice, his cheeks reddening. "It's a bit silly, really, but it gets the job done."

"Sounds cool." Ryan ripped another beer can from the plastic ring and tossed it to Damon. "I think my mum used to have some of the VHS tapes when I was a kid."

Damon sat in the armchair next to the window, and Claire took the right corner of the small, hard sofa. She had been trying to warm Damon up to the idea of hanging out with Ryan for a while, but Damon had insisted 'guys like him' – which she could only imagine meant guys with muscles – didn't like men like *him*.

While the storm raged on over the next few hours, they talked about anything and everything. The laughter only grew as they emptied the small cans of warm lager. Much to Claire's relief, Damon loosened up, warming to Ryan. Despite his slightly intimidating bulky exterior these days, Ryan was (and had always been) one of those guys with whom it was incredibly easy to get along and, more importantly, laugh with. He'd never taken himself too seriously, and Claire was glad adulthood hadn't changed that as it had done for so many people she knew from her youth. A glance at social media told her all she needed to know about how cynical and judgemental her peers could be these days.

"There he goes," Claire said, nodding at Damon as his eyes fluttered shut, one hand still wrapped around the can balanced on his rising and falling stomach. "That'll be him gone until one of us shakes him awake. He sleeps like the dead."

"He's pretty cool."

"I'm glad you think so," she replied, offering him a relieved smile. "He's been a really good friend to me for a long time."

"Are you two . . ."

Ryan's voice drifted off before he sipped his beer, and he darted a suggestive glance at Damon.

"You sound like my mother," she said even as she shook her head. "We hit it off as friends too quickly to ever go there. I think it's crossed everyone's minds but ours. Why'd you ask?"

"You really get on," he said, smiling down into his drink. "You're well-matched."

"Because we're both fat?"

He pursed his lips. "You know that's not what I—"

"I'm kidding," she said with a wink. "We really get on, but we don't see each other like that. I know it's baffling for some people to grasp, but men and women can be friends."

"Like us."

Claire smiled her agreement, but her gaze fixed on the coffee table so she wouldn't have to meet his eyes. After Ryan left, she had occasionally wondered if Damon was merely filling the gap Ryan left behind. Over the years, their friendship blossomed into something unique.

She never fell in love with Damon.

Not as she'd done with Ryan.

Even on the day she watched Ryan drive away from the cul-de-sac without any intention of returning, she couldn't bring herself to confess how she felt for him. Seventeen years later, she still struggled to acknowledge any potential feelings remaining – and perhaps transferring – from her teenage years. How could she? Between his divorce, his kids, his job, and living in a bed and breakfast, Ryan's plate was full. He didn't need another complication, so Claire kept her feelings to herself like she always had.

"Storm seems to be calming down," Ryan pointed out, breaking the silence before draining another can of beer. "Might be a good time to make a run for it."

Claire glanced at her phone. Somehow, it was already a little past eleven. She'd been yawning for the past half an hour but hadn't wanted to move. Despite the location, it had been nice to sit in the cloud of vanilla from the flickering candle and talk with nothing but the sound of the storm. Sighing a little, she finished her second can and stood.

"I'll put some more water and biscuits down for Pickles until I figure out what to do with him." She yawned and stretched. "Don't suppose you want a cat?"

"Amelia has been nagging for one since we moved here." He stood and did a little stretching of his own. "Might be the straw that breaks the camel's back at the B&B though."

"Still no luck?"

"I viewed a place on the other side of the farm yesterday," he said, crossing the room. "Well within my budget, but the entire place was covered in damp and stank like an old church." His forehead puckered. "Might not have much choice soon. Jeanie is in our corner, but I get the feeling Agnes is chomping at the bit to see the back of us." He stepped onto the bottom step and said, "Bathroom?"

"First door on the left."

Pickles wasn't in the kitchen, but he'd cleared most of the biscuits. She emptied out the rest of the box and topped up the water, leaving him enough to get through the next day at least. With two cats of her own and about to move into the small flat above her shop,

Claire couldn't take him, but she was determined to find him a good home. She made a mental note to let Sally know he was there.

Thinking of Sally, she remembered the favour her friend had asked her. She looked around the kitchen and dining room for any signs of Uncle Pat's belongings, but aside from the door in the corner, the living areas seemed very much communal and intentionally devoid of any individual personality. Without even realising she was doing it, she drifted upstairs in search of Pat's bedroom.

Though Claire wasn't sure which bedroom her uncle had claimed, an open door soon answered her question. Even from the outside, she recognised that it was his room; it still smelt like the aftershave he used to wear. Pickles was curled up, fast asleep, in the middle of the neatly made bed. He opened one lazy eye as Claire pushed the door open, but he didn't move from his comfy spot. On the dresser, over a dozen framed pictures huddled together.

Next door, the toilet flushed.

Claire reached out and picked up a picture of she and Uncle Pat on holiday in Gran Canaria, posed on a wall in front of the dark sea, faces shiny and tanned, wearing identical, relaxed smiles. Claire had been thirteen during that family holiday, and aside from her much shorter hair now, she barely looked different. Her memories of that specific holiday had always been fond. She even remembered the picture; it didn't take much to conjure the image of her mother and father on the other side of the disposable wind-on camera.

"Thought I heard someone come up," Ryan said, wiping his damp hands down the back of his shorts. "Everything alright?"

"Sally asked me to look through his stuff to see if I wanted to take anything," she said, looking around the room. "It doesn't feel right that I'm even in here, but. . ."

Claire's voice trailed off, and she clutched the picture to her chest, immediately angry at herself for feeling sympathetic towards her uncle. She returned it to the dresser and stepped back to take them all in. Her stomach lurched. Each picture included Uncle Pat and some combination of Claire, her father, her gran, and her mother. There were two more pictures from the Vegas trip with Nick (faces intact), but the rest were strictly family snaps from decades of memories.

"I never questioned why my uncle tagged along for most of our family holidays," she said, frowning deeply. "We were all he had. Isn't it obvious? He never married, never had kids, but he always had us. Used to drive my mum crazy that he was always showing up, but I loved him being there. I loved him like he was my second..."

She stopped herself and swallowed past the lump in her throat.

"It's alright, mate," Ryan said, giving her shoulder a squeeze. "There's no rule book for how you're supposed to feel."

"I wish there were," she said, letting out a sigh. "I don't think I can leave these to go in the skip. I know what he did was awful, but this was his life." She looked down at the picture, and a single tear fell onto the glass – she wiped it away on her thigh immediately. "Beer's making me all mushy. Just ignore me."

"He's still your uncle," Ryan said, squeezing even harder. "The memories you have are still real. Take them."

"What would I even do with them?"

"Figure that out later." He gave her a small hug with one arm. "If I could go back, I'd keep more of my mum's stuff. I know it's not the same situation, but you can't run from the memories. Not in a village like this." He let go and opened the bedroom door. "I'll go and look for a bag while you figure out what you want to do."

Claire stared at the pictures for a minute before finally beginning to stack them. Most of the images were from the period after her birth, so even if she didn't appear in one of the snaps from the many holidays, weddings, birthday parties, and Christmas mornings, she'd been in the room. Aside from the Nick pictures, there was only one she couldn't claim to have witnessed, but she recognised it well. Dressed in pyjamas, Alan and Pat grinned with an arm around each other in front of a decorated tree on Christmas morning, 1966. A copy of the picture had lived on her parents' mantlepiece until recently; she had no idea what her father had done with it.

"Recognise this?" Ryan held up a gym bag as he returned. "I think this is the one Nick had in the video." He ripped it open to show her the contents. "Gym clothes, water bottle, deodorant, but no spray paint."

"He could have ditched it?"

"Maybe." He pulled out the can of deodorant and showed her the red cap. "You don't think—"

"That we added two and two together and came out with forty-seven?" she interrupted, taking the can from him to drop it. Even on the wooden floorboards, it clattered loudly like a can of paint would. "I didn't want to believe my uncle when he said he didn't put Nick up to ruining my shop the night before my launch, and I think this definitely is the beer talking, but I did. I believed him. I can't help it, and that probably makes me a gullible fool, but I believed him."

Claire pulled the contents out of the gym bag and stuffed in the stack of frames before zipping it up.

"If it wasn't Nick," Ryan said, looking around the empty room, "and your uncle wasn't involved, who could have done it?"

"You want to know the truth?" She gulped, locking eyes with Ryan. "I honestly have no idea. But whoever it is must really hate me." She tossed the bag over her shoulder and left the room. "C'mon, let's wake Damon and get out of here. I've seen enough."

AFTER VIOLENTLY SHAKING DAMON TO STIR HIM FROM his slumber, they put their empty cans in the recycling bin under the sink. Once they'd returned the place to the state they found it, they crept out the front door.

While the rain was still heavy, the wind had passed with the worst of the storm, so running away from Christ Church Square wasn't as ferocious as running to it had been. When they reached the B&B, Damon split off in the direction of the village square after a quick hug.

"Come in," Ryan said, already guiding Claire up the stone steps to the front door. "I'm not having you run home in this. There should still be a couple of taxis driving around this time of night."

Once again soaked to the bone, Claire didn't argue. They burst through the open front door to a chilling, high-pitched scream that made the inside no calmer than the outside. Pulling off her water-spotted glasses, Claire squinted up the stairs to the source of the noise. As she wiped the glass on the hem of the soaked, borrowed t-shirt, a black blob flew backwards up the stairs, thrashing and screaming.

"*Agnes*!" Ryan cried, rushing at the shape. "What do you think you're doing!"

Claire crammed on her glasses. The black blob was nine-year-old Amelia in a set of dark pyjamas, and she wasn't flying up the stairs, Agnes was dragging her.

"The child is *feral*!" Agnes cried as she tightened her grip under Amelia's arms and hauled her up the stairs like she was a misbehaving cat on its way to a bath. "I've been trying to get her to go to bed for over two hours, and I've had enough!"

Jeanie rushed into the hallway clutching her cheek,

tears running down her face. Rather than wrapping herself around her father as Ryan freed her, Amelia immediately turned and lashed out at Agnes. Ryan pulled his daughter down the stairs as she kicked and screamed, his grip on her less forceful.

"*Amelia!*" Ryan's usually meek voice boomed with bass as he captured his daughter's flailing arms by her sides. "Calm down. What's going on?"

"*She* hit Jeanie!" Amelia's cheeks were wet with as many tears as Jeanie's as she tried to break free from her father. "She *hit* her!"

A red handprint bloomed beneath Jeanie's fingers. In the distance, more thunder rumbled, letting them know the storm wasn't done with them yet.

"The child *should* have been in bed!" Agnes cried from the top step, hands planted on her hips. Her white, frilly nightie made her slightly less imposing. "How have you been raising this child? She has no respect for anyone!"

"That's no reason to physically drag her up the stairs," Claire said.

Agnes glared at her, but Claire only lifted her chin and refused to look away. She'd had her own run-ins with Agnes. The B&B owner had been at the head of a vocal minority who couldn't bear the thought of Jane's Tearoom becoming a candle shop. Since Claire had played a significant role in solving Jane's murder, she'd assumed they'd called a truce; Agnes' snarling lip disabused her of that belief.

"I'm going to bed," Agnes said, turning with a shake of her head. "I want you three out by morning."

"*Morning?*" Ryan scoffed, opening his arms before Amelia wrapped herself around his neck. "I'm not staying here another night."

Agnes disappeared into the dark without turning back.

"Please, Ryan," Jeanie said, forcing a laugh as she wiped away her tears. "It needn't come to this. Why don't we sit down over a nice cup of tea and sort this out?"

Ryan held Amelia out at arm's length and rubbed at her cheeks with his thumbs.

"Does it hurt anywhere?" he asked her, to which she shook her head. "What were you doing out of bed?"

"They were arguing."

"This is so *silly!*" Jeanie cried. "Agnes will have calmed down by morning, and we can all get back to—"

"I'm sorry, Jeanie," Ryan said, hoisting Amelia onto his hip as if she were still a toddler. "You've been good to us, but we've clearly overstayed our welcome.

There's a chain hotel not too far away. I'll be back in the morning to settle my bill."

"You're staying with me," Claire insisted as she followed him up the stairs. "My parents' guest bedroom has more than enough space. Mum's been looking for an excuse to show it off since she redecorated."

Ryan settled Amelia in the twin room she shared with Hugo. Hugo stirred a little, his game console shining brightly on his pillow next to his head. Ryan picked it up and turned it off before pulling the covers up to his chin and kissing him softly on the forehead. He tried to get Amelia back into bed, but she was already dragging her suitcase out from underneath. He helped her lift it onto the mattress, kissed her on the top of the head, and they left her to empty the chest of drawers. Claire liked seeing this side of Ryan.

"She's not a bad kid," he said as they walked down the dark hall towards Ryan's bedroom. "Her entire life has been uprooted, and she doesn't know how to deal with it. *I* don't know how to deal with it. She misses her mum, any kid would, but how can I possibly explain that I can't just get her here."

"Still no contact?"

"Nothing." He unlocked his door and pushed it open into the dark. "I've called everyone I can think of back in Spain. Maya's dropped off the face of the planet since she ran off with *him*."

In Ryan's tone, Claire heard a similar inflexion to the one she heard in her own voice whenever she talked about Pat. Sometimes, it was easy to forget that everyone had monsters in the closet they were avoiding. Ryan's happened to be Will, the man his wife ran off with to start a new life minus her family. Speaking the man's name would have been difficult in any circumstances, but Ryan's were worse. Will had been Ryan's only close friend even after all his years in Spain. Ryan rarely mentioned either of them.

"The honeymoon period will wear off eventually," Claire said, following him into the dark room. "She'll come to her senses and realise what she's given up."

"I hope so, for their sake."

Aside from the few shirts hanging in the wardrobe, Ryan had never stopped living out of his cases and bags, so packing up took less than half an hour. After making the bed, Ryan gave the drawers a quick scan. He pulled the easel (now empty) out from behind the wardrobe, flicked off the table lamp, and, loaded with cases and bags, joined Claire in the hall without so much as a backwards glance.

Amelia and Hugo were just as ready, fully dressed and sitting on the edge of their bed, eyes drooping.

Ryan ran downstairs to dump his luggage by the door before sprinting up to grab Amelia and Hugo's cases.

"Who's Joey?" Amelia asked after her father left the room.

"Sorry?" Claire asked.

"Jo-ey," she repeated with a roll of her eyes. "Agnes and Jeanie were arguing about him when I went downstairs. They know what he did."

"They know what *Joey* did?" Claire asked, stepping into the room. "That's what you heard?"

"*You know what Joey did!*" Amelia cried, mimicking Agnes' deep tone. "And then she slapped Jeanie." She recreated the movement with her hand in the space between her and Hugo; her brother jumped back, suddenly wide-eyed and awake. "*Wham!* Right across the face!"

Ryan walked back in, slotting his phone into his pocket.

"Taxi will be here in five," he said, beckoning for Amelia and Hugo to leave the room. "Got everything?"

"Triple-checked," Hugo said quietly as he plodded out of the room. "Hi, Claire."

"Hi, kiddo."

Amelia and Hugo led the way downstairs, followed by Ryan. While they went straight to the door to wait with the bags and cases, Claire detoured into the sitting room. In a rocking chair by the window, Jeanie knitted something long and pink, fingers moving with machine precision and speed. Her eyes, meanwhile, stared at nothing.

"What did Joey do?" Claire asked bluntly.

Jeanie's eyes snapped to Claire's, and the knitting needles stopped their clacking. Her lips parted, but before she could speak, her brow furrowed. She looked away from Claire, focusing on her knitting. The needles and wool resumed their progress, albeit slower and more intentional.

"What's that, dear?"

"What did Joey do?"

"I don't think I know a Joey, dear." Jeanie kicked the floor and the chair rocked. "Sorry, love."

"My mistake."

Claire left the sitting room and joined the kids at the front door while Ryan dashed out into the rain to load the taxi waiting by the kerb. Scooping up a pile of the black bags containing Ryan's clothes, she ran out after him. She dumped the bags in the boot and turned back to the B&B as Ryan led the kids out through the front door. Jeanie watched from behind the net curtain.

Claire had always liked Jeanie, but she didn't doubt that the B&B owner had just barefaced lied to her. She might not have got out of her what Joey had done, but the look of horror in her eyes had confirmed Amelia's young ears hadn't betrayed her.

Joey had done something, all right, and Claire's new mission was to figure out what.

CHAPTER TEN

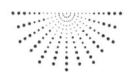

Although surprised to have guests so late, a nightie-clad Janet launched into a hosting scenario Claire could only imagine she'd been waiting a lifetime to play out based on how quickly everything was done. Within five minutes of the taxi turning up, Ryan, Amelia, and Hugo were settled by the roaring fire in the sitting room with drinks and a selection of biscuits. After what sounded like a frenzied rush to strip and replace the bedding in the guest bedroom, Janet came down, fully clothed.

"The bed is ready," she said softly, her sweet perfume twinkling in from the hall. "It's a king-size, so it'll fit the three of you for one night. I've left towels and a selection of toiletries on the bed. I also left little chocolates on your pillows but try not to eat them while *in* bed."

As expected, the little family tromped straight upstairs. Claire followed soon after, far too tired to explain everything to her mother. She fed her cats extra by way of apology for being home so late, stripped off her still damp clothes, and crawled into bed wearing her softest, fluffiest pyjamas. She planned to pretend to be asleep when her mother inevitably walked in to demand answers in the shout-whisper voice she used whenever they had guests, but the soft rain pattering on the windowpane was too enticing to ignore.

Claire awoke to the sound of sparkling birdsong, with Domino curled up on one side, and Sid stretched out on the other. She performed a little stretch of her own and smiled when she opened her eyes and saw the crystal-blue sky through the gap in the curtains. She enjoyed a moment with the cats, their soft purrs the perfect morning greeting. Already in a good mood, she sat up, ready to start another day at the shop.

Only when something smashed downstairs did Claire remember the guests. She climbed out of bed, fed the cats, scooped out their litter, and hurried down in her pyjamas and slippers. Janet was in the kitchen, wiping up what appeared to be a mushy pile of cornflakes and the shattered pieces of the best china reserved for guests.

"Just a little accident!" she exclaimed, blowing her hair out of her face as she swept up the mess. "We're having breakfast al fresco this morning."

"Butterfingers, butterfingers!" Amelia chanted as she ran around her brother. Both already wore their school uniforms – a red jumper with a white polo shirt. It hadn't changed since Claire and Ryan attended the same school as children. "Hugo's clumsy! Hugo's clumsy!"

"Shut up." He pushed her away. "It was an accident."

"Just an accident!" Janet said again as she dumped the contents of the dustpan into the bin. "No harm done! Now, run along outside and get yourselves seated at the table. Claire, a word." She waited until they were outside before dragging Claire into the kitchen. "What is going on? And before you say 'nothing,' I know *something* is, girl! Does this have anything to do with Nick?"

"Ryan being here?"

"No, you acting all weird!" She swatted Claire lightly with a tea towel. "You're running around, sneaking off here and there. What's this I heard about a six-hour dentist appointment? You have responsibilities! You don't just get to drop the shop when you feel like going off to Manchester to get drunk with your hippie friend." Janet nodded, clearly pleased with herself. "Oh yes, I pay attention, dear. I see things. I saw you waiting at the bus stop yesterday morning."

"I went to see Uncle Pat," she said, leaning in. "Weren't expecting that, were you?"

Janet's jaw dropped, her gaze going straight to Claire's father in the garden, where he read his paper while the kids played footsie under the table.

"Have you gone *mad*?" she hissed, pushing Claire into the hallway and closing the door behind them. "How could you do such a thing?"

"Because I'm beginning to think everyone *else* has gone mad!" Claire fired back. "I can't even say Pat's name without" – Claire paused as her mother shuddered – "people wincing. He's not Voldemort!"

"Who's that?"

"From *Harry Potter*?"

"You know I can't stand witches and wizards, dear."

"The point is, we can't pretend he doesn't exist or that he didn't do what he did." Claire glanced at the wall towards Graham's cottage. "We live next door to a constant reminder!" She paused and inhaled to calm herself. "I know Dad has been sneaking my letters, and from the way you two have been lately, I think you know it, too."

"He knows you know," she whispered, resting a hand on her head. "Steaming the letters?"

"He knows?"

"*Really*, Claire?" She pursed her lips. "Don't insult your father's intelligence. You think a retired detective inspector wouldn't notice? And besides, you put them back in the wrong drawer!"

"Damon did."

"Oh!" Janet snapped her fingers together. "The *Scrabble*! I should have known. I see the text messages you send me. You can't spell at the best of times." Her brows tilted, fear crossing her face. "Why did you visit him, Claire?"

"Because I thought he was behind the vandalism of my shop."

"Thought?" Janet rolled her eyes. "He *is*! The video proved it! He's twisting your mind, Claire. He wants to use you to wriggle his way back into our good graces. He knows you'll fall for it!"

"I'm not a kid, Mum!"

"You *act* like one!"

"And you don't?" Claire planted her hands on her hips, mirroring her mother's posture. "Stomping around, giving each other the silent treatment, avoiding talking about the one thing we should all be talking about? It's—"

Claire stopped when she heard the upstairs bathroom door close. Ryan appeared at the top of the stairs, dressed for a day at work, with his ginger hair wet and hanging over his eyes like he used to wear it when they were kids.

"Morning," he said.

"*Morning!*" they replied in the same fake, high-pitched tone.

"Something smells good," he said, spinning around the bannister.

"Breakfast is al fresco in the garden." Janet opened the kitchen door, and rather than remaining in the hall to argue with Claire, she went back to cleaning up the mess from the dropped bowl.

Claire ate breakfast in almost complete silence, barely able to look at her father. Knowing he knew that she knew he'd been hiding her mail was embarrassing enough. The fact that he didn't know she knew that he knew that she'd opened and read the letters was enough to make her head hurt. That conversation, at least, could wait until they didn't have an audience.

Alan stayed behind to clear away the breakfast things as Janet, Ryan, the kids, and Claire loaded into the car. After much fiddling with the seat and the mirrors, Janet set off at her usual snail's pace, dropping Ryan and Claire in the square before taking the kids to Northash Primary School on the edge of the village.

Parting on a promise to have lunch together there, Claire opened her candle shop. Turning the sign and unlocking the door still sent a thrill of excitement through her. Soon, a slow-but-steady stream of customers began trickling through the door. Claire desperately wanted to talk to Granny Greta about the casino, vowing that if Greta didn't come to her, she'd make it her mission to find her when the shop closed. Thankfully, Greta and Spud stopped by on their morning walk a little before eleven.

"C-casino?" she said airily when Claire posed the question. "Where'd you hear about that, then?"

Once Claire had settled her gran in a chair with a cup of tea, she recounted the whole messy affair, beginning with her father's mail-stealing through finally opening the letters, the subsequent prison visit, her visit to Pat's cottage, and, at last, repeating the conversation she'd had with her mother in the hallway that very morning.

"My Alan has always been like this!" Greta announced, slamming her half-finished cup of tea down on the counter. "He had this rabbit, Oliver, which died when he was twelve, and did we dare say the name 'Oliver' ever again? Did we, bugger! Stubborn thing made it impossible. He's a sensitive soul, but he buries his head in the sand like no other. He was the same when your grandfather died."

"But were you part of it, Gran?" Claire asked after pausing to serve a customer who'd bought two of the coconut milk candles. She lowered her voice. "The . . . card ring?"

"Oh, you make it sound so *nefarious*!" Greta tutted. "It was just a bit of fun for a couple of quid. Your uncle came back from Vegas with lights in his eyes, so we set up a little club. The jackpots were tiny. Hundred quid if we were lucky. It was just for a laugh! Quite a few people got involved, but we had to keep it hush-hush." She tapped her nose, leaned in and whispered, "Especially from your father. Not quite legal, you see, but we were doing no harm. It was Pat's little passion project. He wasn't in it to make money."

One of the customers glanced over her shoulder at Greta, left her basket, and went straight for the door.

"Stopped being fun when Pat was taken away," she continued, in a louder voice now that the shop was empty. "Nick carried it on, and I went a couple of times, but it wasn't the same. He kept upping the stakes. Half the club dropped out then and there, but a couple stayed. I guess they liked the rush."

The shop door opened and Em walked in, her rainbow tie-dye shorts as bright as the afternoon sun behind her. Em went straight to greeting Spud, and while she stroked him, Claire caught her up on everything she'd learned.

"That lines up with what I overheard yesterday," Em said, rising to lean against the doorframe to the back room. "Gwyneth didn't say much. Pretended like she didn't know about the casino and couldn't think of any reason why anyone would want to murder Nick. I know I said she'd never lie to me, but I could feel her lying. I took my dad's dog for a walk around Starfall Park right before the storm hit, and who did I find but Gwyn and Joey walking around the Chinese garden. Gwyneth was crying hysterically, and Joey was trying to calm her down, but she ended up pushing him so hard he fell. Gwyneth was talking about 'gambling too big' and saying she 'knew this would happen.' Then they saw me and both went their separate ways before I could say anything to either of them."

"They're definitely in on it!" Greta proclaimed, tapping Claire and pointing at Em. "Tell her what you overheard at the B&B."

"Technically, Amelia overheard it," she said,

glancing around the empty shop. "From the sounds of it, Joey has done *something*, and it was bad enough to have Agnes and Jeanie arguing. Agnes slapped Jeanie across the face. Her cheek was red raw."

"Poor Jeanie!"

"I asked her about Joey," she continued. "She pretended like she didn't even know him."

"That's a load of toffee!" Greta laughed. "Jeanie was still there when Joey joined the club. I don't think Jeanie stayed long after me, but Joey showed up the second week after Nick took over. That's the time I stopped going."

"I thought Joey and Nick hated each other."

"Nick never hated anyone," Em said with a sideways smile. "When it came to money, he took advantage, but he always tried to pay his debts in the end. He wasn't malicious. Joey hated Nick, but I know Nick never resented him. I suspect he even thought Joey was the better option for Gwyneth, but she couldn't seem to keep away."

"Women like her always go for the bad boys," Greta said. "The question is, did Joey finally want Gwyneth all to himself? Could *he* have killed Nick? Is that what he did?"

"I don't think Joey would be capable," Em said, though her voice wavered with uncertainty.

"No offence, love," Greta said, tapping Em on the arm, "but my son used to trap spiders under glasses rather than killing them, and now he's in prison for murdering two human beings. He let his monster in. You're old enough to know we all have one. We're all only one mistake away from ruining our lives."

Claire's ears pricked up at the words alarmingly like the ones she'd heard from her uncle. Once Em left to get to her first yoga session of the day, Claire turned to her gran and raised her eyebrows.

"You visited him too. He told me the exact same line about letting the monster in."

"He didn't say it to me, dear," Greta said, rising to her feet, "I said it to him. I couldn't not visit my son. No matter what he's done."

"He never mentioned it."

"I asked him not to." Greta smiled wryly before plodding off to the door with Spud at her heels. "I knew you'd go eventually, I was just waiting for you to pluck up the courage to read his letters."

"You knew about them?"

"Your father keeps no secrets from me," she said, pausing at the door. "Not these days. I make sure of it. I let one son slip through my fingers, I won't lose another. Just know it's been eating him up as much as you think it has, and the sooner you're both honest with each other, the better. Talk to him, Claire. I won't put up with this for much longer."

Feeling suitably told off, Claire felt a fool for believing the letters were as secret as she had assumed. It brought her some comfort to know her father had confided in his mother, at least. Still, it didn't make his reason behind keeping them so secret any more comfortable to face, especially now each knew the other was hiding something.

After Sally dropped by between property viewings to pick up the keys to the cottage, Ryan came around with the promised chippy lunch.

"I've been thinking," she said as they picked at the salt and vinegar soaked chips during the lunchtime lull. "I'm not using the flat above this place yet. It's basically sitting empty until I can gather the strength to attack building all that furniture. If we got the bed up tonight, you'd have somewhere to sleep that's a little more private, at least."

"It's your flat, Claire," he said, his pale cheeks blushing red. "You've already done enough."

"And yet I can do more. I'm not taking no for an answer, mate. My parents can put up with me until you find the perfect house. You have two kids, and I have two cats. It's hardly fair, is it?"

"But it's your dream."

"*This* is my dream." She motioned around the shop. "The flat was always a bonus. Gives me an excuse to put off ironing my own clothes for a little while longer. Besides, it's temporary. Sally was in earlier, and I asked her to make finding you the perfect place in your price range her top priority. If anyone can, it's her."

"Thanks, mate." He reached across the counter and rested his hand on hers. "It's . . . it's nice to know you have my back."

Ryan stayed for the duration of his lunch break, and by the time he left, the shop was already filling up again. By two, Claire had experienced her busiest rush since opening day, and by closing at five, she felt like she'd finally put her first real day running the shop on her own behind her.

She'd also managed to write down everything she knew about Nick and the people surrounding him. Each thread either went back to money or Gwyneth, but neither tangent felt like it was painting a full picture.

As Claire was locking up the shop, Joey hurried past. He wore another ill-fitting suit, this time with a bright yellow shirt and shocking pink tie. Not wanting to miss an opportunity, Claire caught up with him before he reached Lilac Gifts.

"Can I have a word?" Claire said, half-jogging to keep up with his pace.

"I'm busy."

"It'll only take a minute."

"If you want to speak to Gwyneth, you can—"

"It's actually *you* that I want to speak to."

Claire stepped around Joey before he reached the door to Gwyneth's shop. He glared down at her, tossing back his lank combover with a lazy throw of his head. Claire hadn't prepared questions for him, but that hardly mattered. Looking into his eyes, she knew he wouldn't answer a single one.

Instead, she reached for a different tactic.

"I know what you did," she said firmly, narrowing her eyes at him. "I *know*."

The lawyer's firm demeanour melted, and as the veneer slipped away, someone emerged who better matched the version Em talked about from her school days. His eyebrows tilted and bottom lip wobbled as he searched Claire's eyes. The words seemed jammed in his throat, but before any came, he pushed past her into the shop.

In calling his bluff, Claire had got a reaction more than anything she'd bargained for. She'd expected the shock, but not to see such horror in his eyes.

It was familiar.

She'd seen a glimmer of the same in Jeanie's eyes the previous night.

She'd seen the look in Uncle Pat's eyes, too, right after she'd accused him of murder.

"*Claire?*" DI Ramsbottom called from behind as he clambered out of his tiny red car. "What a small world. I've just come from your house, and here you are, outside my niece's shop as I'm on my way to see her!"

"Before you do," Claire said quietly, "how about a slice of cake at Marley's? My treat."

CHAPTER ELEVEN

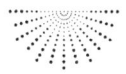

Around the corner in Marley's Café, Claire watched DI Ramsbottom devour his slice of carrot cake in mere seconds. She pushed hers towards him, and he accepted it with wriggly fingers, proclaiming he hadn't had a chance to eat since lunch. Neither had Claire, but the unsettling look in Joey's eyes had left her without an appetite.

"So, let me get this straight," Ramsbottom said as he crammed in a mouthful of her cake. "You think Joseph has done something bad – but you don't know what – based on the evidence of strange looks and the testimony of a nine-year-old girl? And it's all connected to some casino being run in a cellar? It's hardly going to hold up in court, is it?"

"I know that," Claire said, a little too curtly. "That's

why we're in the local café and not at the station. I have nothing concrete to go on, but it's been days since Nick's death, and what else do you have to work with?"

The door opened. A group of teenagers wearing unfamiliar school uniforms strolled in and took a table in the middle of the empty café, providing a natural buffer between Claire's table and the counter. While Marley walked over to take their orders, Eugene, his husband, stood on tiptoes, not even trying to hide that he'd been listening to every word of Claire's theory.

"To be fair to us, we only launched a murder case yesterday," Ramsbottom mumbled through the last bite of cake, sending tiny orange pieces flying. "We thought Nick's case was as good as solved. A simple suicide! Well, not simple, but you know what I mean. Cut and dry." He dabbed at the corners of his mouth with a napkin before scrunching it onto the double-stacked empty plates. "Now the pathologist is saying he was strangled, and it's got us on the back foot. But *you* think you're on the right one with this Joey theory?"

Claire sipped her coffee, unsure if she was on any foot at all. Strange looks and the statement of a nine-year-old weren't much. Instead of pulling on the right thread, it was like the jumper had entirely unravelled, leaving her to put it back together with fingers covered in glue.

"I learned all of this by accident," Claire said quietly, glad the teenagers were making a suitable amount of noise with their rising chatter and jeering. "I saw the slap mark on Jeanie's face. I saw the look in her eyes when I brought up Joey. I saw the look in *his* eyes when I called his bluff." She paused to sip her coffee. Even the memory of Joey's expression still made her uneasy. "They're all members of the same little casino, and something's going on."

"I admit," he said with a slightly scrunched nose, "I did know about that. Gwyneth tried to get me involved. Poor lass didn't realise it was technically illegal, so I declined and told her I'd look the other way. She said they were playing for a pound or two. Nothing major."

"From the sounds of it, Nick had a serious gambling issue," she confessed. "He was in the bookies the day before he died, gambling away thousands he borrowed from his brother."

"Another suspect!" Ramsbottom pulled his notepad and pen from his pocket and started scribbling. "That's the fella from the taxi rank, isn't it?"

"Ste," she confirmed before adding, "He gave me the details about the casino. He only went to one meeting, and he didn't seem to know what was going on."

"Could be lying?" he suggested, lowering the pad briefly. "Throwing you off the scent?"

"Maybe."

"And if his brother borrowed money off him?" Ramsbottom added a few more notes. "The perfect motive."

"I suppose," she said, frowning. "But it's Joey you need to be finding out about first. Everything seems to be swirling around this casino club Nick was running. Joey was part of it, and so was your niece. Something is going on there, and it's a start, Detective."

"I've never trusted Joey, to tell you the truth." He scratched at his artificially shiny hair. "Slimy sort of fella and I don't trust lawyers at the best of times. I've seen guilty people wriggle out of serious charges with the right lawyer. He's never been right for Gwyn. Too possessive. There's a reason you don't stay with who you courted in school. I wouldn't be surprised if he killed Nick to finally get my niece all to himself, and that's before taking into account everything you've told me about their little underground gambling ring." He paused, biting into his lip. "I hope my Gwyneth isn't in any trouble."

"It's just a hunch." Claire sipped her coffee, cleared

her throat, and added in a sugary voice, "Everyone knows you're the best DI around. If anyone can figure it out, it's you."

At the counter, Eugene choked on his tea before letting out a booming cough. Marley tutted loudly as he turned the television up to give them more privacy from listening ears. Claire smiled gratefully.

"People say that?" he asked in a low voice, leaning in. "The *best?*"

"The best," she lied.

"Hmmm." Ramsbottom nodded, visibly inflating with pride in front of her. "Maybe I should start with the B&B sisters? Find out what they know about what Joey's allegedly done?"

"That's where I'd start," she agreed. "I'd be there right now if I thought either of them would talk to me. Agnes has had it in for me since I dared to change the status quo of the tearoom, and Jeanie seems too embarrassed by what I walked in on to ever talk to me again."

"Sometimes a little official pressure loosens tongues," he said, patting his jacket pocket – she imagined his badge must be hidden in there. "Not your uncle's tongue, mind. Went to see him today to put the graffiti case to rest, and I couldn't get him to crack. He's a good actor, I'll give him that. Said you'd visited?"

"I suppose I didn't tell him to keep it a secret," she said, looking through the window to Greta's cottage at the bottom of the street. "For what it's worth, I don't think it was him after all."

"You don't?" Ramsbottom arched a brow and it vanished under the floppy front of his toupee. "But the video? The spray paint?"

"It could have been a can of deodorant," she said, pausing to wonder how she could say she'd seen inside the bag without confessing to being in the cottage for much of the previous night. "Maybe have the video looked at?"

He scribbled down another line of notes. When he was done, he stabbed the pen on the page one last time before flipping his notebook shut and putting it away.

"You know, you're just like your father," he said. "You have the same mind. It's uncanny."

Claire smiled, the comparison was the biggest compliment anyone could pay her. It only made her feel guiltier about not talking to him about any of this. Her gran's warning echoing in her ears, she pushed out her chair.

"Time to face the music," she said, motioning to Marley for the bill as she pulled out her card. "I hope my tips were helpful, Detective Inspector. I'd be interested to hear if you find anything."

"Of course," he said, tapping his nose. "Strictly off the record, though."

After paying, she left the café, declining Ramsbottom's invitation for a lift home in his comically tiny car. She was sceptical they would both fit, and she needed the walk to try and figure out how she could approach things with her father without sending him scurrying for his shed. Besides, after the day before, she wanted to enjoy the warm sun and lovely breeze.

By the time she passed it, Lilac Gifts was closed for the day. Claire would have given anything to be a fly on the wall for whatever conversation Joey and Gwyneth were currently having. She wondered if Gwyneth knew what Joey had done. Sweet as she was, Gwyneth denying her role in the casino club proved that, like everyone, she was capable of lying. If she did know about Joey's indiscretion, Claire expected Gwyneth to cover for him. They'd known each other since school, after all, and Claire understood all too well how strong that bond could be.

On her way across the square, she peered into the still-open gym. Jeanie's knitted cardigan and the scarf covering her roller-filled hair was as out of place in the gym as Claire usually looked. Ryan was on the other side of the glass counter, his back to the door. His arms were folded and his spine ramrod straight, while Jeanie leant across the glass, her face pleading. Claire waited outside until Jeanie rushed out. Though she glanced at Claire, she didn't linger.

"Practically begged me to go back to the B&B," Ryan explained when Claire approached. "From the sounds of it, my living there for so long has been keeping the lights on."

"Would you?"

He shook his head. "Agnes and Amelia have rubbed each other the wrong way since the day we moved in. It was only a matter of time before that powder keg exploded. She's out of control."

"Agnes?"

"Amelia." He paused to rub at his forehead. "I'm failing her as a father, Claire. It's so easy with Hugo, and yet I can't seem to get on her wavelength. It's like she hates me."

"She doesn't hate you." Claire reached across the counter and rested her hand on his folded arms. "Take it from the daughter of a good father, it's obvious that girl adores you. You said it last night: she's going through a tough time. You all are."

"I just wish I could help her channel these feelings she's having."

"How did your mother deal with you when your dad left?"

"Painting," he said without hesitation. "She sat me down and forced me to paint with her. I hated it. At least until I started to get quite good, and then I fell in love."

Claire smiled. "I think you've found your answer."

"You think?" He scratched at the back of his head. "I'm not *that* good. I'm rusty after all these years. I don't think I'd be an excellent teacher."

"Ryan, she's nine." Claire chuckled, patting him on the shoulder. "You can learn together. She was colouring in those books the night before I opened. I bet she'd love it. Something for the two of you."

"You're right," he said, finally smiling. "Thanks, mate. Is your offer of the flat still on the table?"

"I wasn't taking no for an answer."

"Then give me ten minutes," he said, checking the clock on the wall. "I'll get this place cleared out, and we can get started on that flatpack."

"Make it an hour," she said, already heading for the door. "I need to go home and be a good daughter myself."

Claire walked through the sliding doors and set off for the lane, only for the car her parents shared to pull out of the carpark concealed behind the row of shops housing Lilac Gifts. Thankfully, only her mother was in the car. Janet lurched to a halt and wound down the passenger window.

"Get in," she said. "You're coming home. Now."

"I was already on my way. I fancied the walk, actually, if you—"

"Your father knows." Janet reached out and pushed open the door, snapping for Claire to get in. "He's just been on the phone asking about you visiting Pat in prison. I played dumb, but he knows."

"*What?*" Claire jumped into the car. "No, no, *no*! I didn't want it to happen like this. I was going to tell him now. That's why I was going home."

"Well, someone got there first." Janet set off up the lane towards the cul-de-sac. "It was bound to happen, Claire. You must have told someone with a big mouth!"

"Only Em, Ryan, and Sally know," she said. "And gran. And you."

"Who *didn't* you tell?"

"DI Ramsbottom," she said, wincing. "He found out from Pat. When we had coffee just now, he'd just been to see Dad. He must have said something not realising it was a secret."

"That's your problem!" Janet cried. "What's with all the secrets all of a sudden?"

"Can we just drive in silence."

"Really, Claire?"

"Yes."

"I'm only saying," she muttered. "We never kept secrets from each other, that's all."

"We also didn't have a murderer in the family."

To Claire's surprise, her bluntness was all it took to get the silence she wanted. Her head spun as she scrambled for the pathetic excuses she'd give for not being open with her father. Technically, he'd started it, and her only real crime was not telling him the truth. She wasn't sure if that was the same as lying, but it made her feel just as bad.

As Janet reversed the car into the parking space in front of their cottage, Claire's phone rang in her handbag. She leaned down to get it in the footwell, smiling and nodding at Graham as he pruned his rose bushes. He tipped his head to her and gave Janet a little wave. She waved right back, her brightest 'everything is wonderful' smile plastered widely from ear to ear.

"It's Sally," she explained as she pressed the green answer button. "Hello, mate. What's up?"

"Must you talk like that?" her mother muttered. "It's so informal."

"Mate?" Sally called down the phone, the echo indicating she was on a loudspeaker. "I've just got to your uncle's place. I thought you said you left it as it was?"

"We did," she replied, turning away from her mother, who didn't know she'd spent the previous night in her uncle's cottage and not at Sally's drinking wine. That was definitely a lie. "Put everything we touched back where it came from. Except for the beer, but we threw the cans in the recycling."

Janet tutted.

"You can go inside, you know," Claire said, resting the phone against her shoulder for a moment before putting it back to her ear. "Everything alright?"

Sally screamed, sounding like she was on the other side of the room.

"Mate?" Claire called. "Sally? You alright?"

But Sally only continued to scream.

"*Drive!*" Claire demanded, slapping the dashboard. "Christ Church Square. I think Sally's in trouble."

"Now I bet you're glad I stayed in the car."

Janet reversed out, her usually slow driving suddenly nippy. She swung the car around the cul-de-sac, mounting the kerb and almost knocking down Graham's fence in the process. She waved an apology before speeding down the lane as fast as the automatic car could take them. They approached the bridge so quickly Claire felt the wheels take momentary flight.

"Now I know why you drive so slowly!"

"I won't take driving advice from someone who failed her test so many times she was on first name terms with *all* the instructors at the test centre."

After a few sharp turns, Janet screeched to a halt in the square, blocking off the rest of the vehicles in the small car park in the process. Claire jumped out and ran straight through the open door and into the middle cottage. Sally was in the kitchen, and she dove on Claire the second she saw her. While Sally hugged her, Claire looked around. The few items in the room were strewn on the floor, all smashed up.

"This is not how I left it," Claire said shakily. "It looks like someone had a fight."

Pickles waltzed in and wrapped himself around Claire's feet a couple of times before sauntering to the now empty biscuit bowl.

"The door was open," Sally said, her shaking finger pointing at the entrance to the casino. "I would never have seen him otherwise."

"Seen who?"

Claire let go of Sally and stepped over Pickles. In the corner, she reached out to push the door all the way open but froze when she saw the smudged bloody fingerprints on the door. Matching ones around the same height on the shiny gloss doorframe. Stepping over the smashed remains of the prototype vanilla candle, she peered down the cellar steps. Two uniformed officers were already down there, and while they were blocking a lot, through the gap of their high-visibility yellow jackets, another bright shade of yellow jumped out.

Joey was up against the door in an awkward position as though he'd fallen down the stairs and landed with his back a little too high against the closed door at the bottom. His eyes were wide, his skin icily pale, and blood stained the left side of his yellow shirt and pink tie.

One of the officers noticed Claire and cleared his throat. The two of them set off up the dark stairway, blocking her view.

She didn't mind.

She had seen enough bodies in this house lately to last her a lifetime.

CHAPTER TWELVE

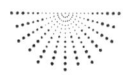

For the second time that evening, Janet reversed into the parking space in front of the cottage. This time, they had Sally in the back. Janet had offered to drive her home to her cottage above the park, but Sally hadn't wanted to 'put on a show' for her husband and kids. She'd accepted Claire's invitation back to the cottage with eagerness.

"You're turning my home into a halfway house," Janet muttered as she hurried to the front door while Sally extricated herself from the car. "Who are you going to invite in next? Mrs Beaton and her army of smelly cats?"

"Oh, you love it, Mother," Claire retorted, overtaking her to get to the front door first. "Don't think I didn't hear you rattling around the bathroom at six this morning. I could smell the bleach from all the way down the hall."

"I just like things to be their best, dear."

"And this is your chance to finally show it off."

Claire headed straight to the wine rack in the kitchen. Though she rarely drank wine at home, red wine was always the beverage of choice for girls' nights at Sally's. At some point over the years, Sally had developed expensive tastes, but Claire barely registered the differences between the labels.

"Not that!" Janet hissed over her shoulder. "That's the good stuff. She can have the cheap plonk on the bottom rack."

"I'll pay you back," she said, already looking for the corkscrew in the cutlery drawer. "I'm gainfully employed now."

"It's two hundred pounds a bottle."

"Cheap plonk it is." She eased the expensive bottle back into the rack, suddenly terrified of dropping it. "What are you buying two hundred quid wine for?"

"It was an anniversary present for your father. He hasn't been in the mood to drink it."

Claire uncorked a bottle and put it down in front of Sally with a glass. If Sally noticed it was 'cheap plonk,' she didn't say. The first glass went down in no time, and she topped it up again.

"He was just lying *there*." Sally gestured with the glass, sloshing wine over the top. Her hands hadn't stopped shaking. "Neck all bent and bleeding like that. He must have fallen hard."

"He was bleeding before he fell," Claire mused aloud, leaning against the island and lifting her gaze thoughtfully towards the ceiling. "I noticed blood on the door and its frame."

Claire crossed to the kitchen door and dragged herself backwards out of the room, clutching the door and frame as she went. "He touched where he was bleeding, so there was blood on his hands. Then someone pushed him, and he fell backwards, grasping for anything to stop the inevitable." She glanced at her fingers and rubbed them together. "The blood will have made them slippery."

"Oh, here she goes," Janet said, pulling two of her giant 'emergency lasagnes' from the freezer. "Always been so melodramatic, dear. You should have done so much better in your drama GCSE. You know she got a D, Sally?" Janet rolled her eyes over the counter as Sally sipped her wine. "What did you get?"

"I took history instead," she replied. "I got an A."

"Of course you did." Janet pursed her lips at Claire, but her expression softened almost at once. "You got there in the end, I suppose."

"A man has just died, and here we are talking about my D in drama from twenty years ago," Claire said, walking back into the kitchen. "Not the first time that's come up recently, actually."

"If there are twelve slices in a baguette," Janet said, pulling out two plastic-wrapped breadsticks, "and there are" – she counted up in her head – "five adults and two children, how many baguettes would I need for everyone to have three slices?" She planted her wrists on her hips with the baguettes pointing out and stared into the freezer. "You know, I'll just cook all six, and if there's leftover, it'll do for pâté later."

Leaving her mother to dither over the cooking, Claire joined Sally at the table. Sally offered a wobbly wine-stained smile before relaxing further into the chair at the dining table.

It was clear Sally wanted to speak, so Claire remained silent, waiting.

Finally, Sally took a deep breath and said, "What was he doing there?"

"The casino in the cellar," Claire said. "He was part of it. I'm guessing he went to meet someone there. Maybe they thought it would be secret? It had to be someone in that club. Who else had keys?"

"We never found Nick's set," Sally confessed after another hearty mouthful of wine. "It's almost funny that the locksmith is booked in to change them tomorrow. One more day and a man might not have died. Who else was in the club?"

"Who wasn't, by the sounds of it. Lately, it's whittled down to Gwyneth, Joey, Agnes, and Nick. And now two of them are dead." Claire shook her head. "Could it be a coincidence that I was led to Nick?"

Sally shrugged, clutching her glass like a lifeline. Leaving her with her drink, Claire followed the sound of her father's voice down the hall and into the living room. To her surprise, he was playing *Scrabble* with Amelia and Hugo. Both still wore their school uniforms. Claire leaned against the doorframe and watched, reflecting their smiles. Her father looked up, and his laughter curdled into dread when he saw her. Claire's smile vanished immediately; her father's expression was almost too much to bear.

"Are you two okay to continue on your own for a little while?"

"Yep." Amelia placed her tiles on the board. "I'm winning anyway, Pops."

Alan ruffled her hair before grabbing his cane and strolling into the hallway. He gave Claire's cheek a little pat as he passed and gestured for her to follow.

"C'mon on, little one. We've lots to discuss, and there's only one place for it."

They headed through the back door and down the path to his gardening shed. He'd always spent time in there over the years, but never more than since his retirement. Claire's mother often joked that if she put a bed and a toilet in there, they'd only ever see him again for feeding or watering.

Alan took his usual seat in the muddy old office chair at the potting desk. Claire perched on the upturned terracotta plant pot that had lived in the corner for her since she was a little girl. She'd never really fit on it, but it was her place; she couldn't imagine ever sitting anywhere else.

"Dad, I'm really—"

"If you're about to apologise, don't." He held up a hand, his expression soft. "It's this silly old man who needs to apologise. I've been a fool. I've been hiding your mail because I was . . . I was . . . "

"You don't have to explain yourself, Dad," Claire said, reaching out to grab his hand tightly in hers. "I understood why you were doing it."

"You do?"

"I found out a while ago," she said, scrunching up her face. "I was letting it happen. In some ways, you were doing me a favour. I wasn't ready to read them until I thought I *had* to. Even though it turns out I was probably barking up the wrong tree, reading those letters was like pulling out a thorn that had been bothering me for ages." She offered a quick, reassuring squeeze. "I know you know, but I did go to see him, and I'm sorry for not telling you."

"Harry mentioned it," he said with a tight smile, confirming Claire's suspicions. "Like I said, little one, you have nothing to apologise for. It's me who must apologise. I'm sorry for making things so unbearable regarding even the mere mention of my brother. I see it on all your faces when I throw my – and let's call them what they are – *tantrums*. And yet, I can't seem to stop myself. It's an instinct. He betrayed us. He betrayed this family. He—"

"Dad, he betrayed himself," she said, clasping his hand hard. "It's not our job to carry his burden. We have to live with it, but *he* made those choices. Not us." She shrugged one shoulder. "We've turned him into the bogeyman, but it's still him. He's still Pat."

For the first time, her father didn't wince. He merely nodded and squeezed her hand back.

"You're absolutely right," he said solemnly. "Now I feel even more foolish for not talking to you sooner. Little one, I *always* knew *you* could handle it. I wasn't sure I could. I did what I thought was best."

"And I love you for that."

"But I also buried my head in the sand. I'm old enough and ugly enough to know where that gets me. Nowhere." He lifted his free hand to the large scar on his head. "If I hadn't ignored the headaches for so long, my foot might still be in good working order." He kissed the back of her hand. "I failed you, Claire, and I'm sorry for that. I should have respected you."

"It's done." Claire wiped away a tear. "Look at us harping on. You know, I know, everyone knows."

"Did you think I'd be mad at you for reading your letters?" he asked, frowning. "Mad at you for visiting your uncle?"

"A little," she admitted.

"Then I really have let all of this carry on for too long." He opened the top drawer – her letters were gone, but there was a new one, addressed to Alan. "This landed on the doormat this morning. Part of me thought I was just going to start a new pile, but . . ." His voice trailed off as he ripped it open. "Like you said, pulling out a thorn."

Alan read over the letter, his lips tracing the words carefully and slowly. When he flipped it, a visiting order fell from his fingers. Claire picked it up. This time, the order was addressed to Alan.

"I thought he was looking for revenge when I saw

that graffiti," Alan said after he finished the letter, his eyes bright with tears. "Before that, I assumed he was looking for redemption because of how insistent he was on trying to contact you. Now, I know my brother is just lonely and ashamed."

"Will you go and see him?"

"I think I have to," he said after a forceful exhale. "Will you come with me, Claire? I'm not sure I fancy the drive to Manchester on my own."

Claire nodded with a teary smile of her own, clutching both of her father's hands in hers. Em had done it for her, and she'd got her through to the other side. Pulling out that thorn taught Claire the pain was temporary. She wasn't sure when the wound would heal, but at least it could.

"Now that it's out in the open," she said, leaning back on the plant pot. "I want to pick your brains about something."

"Ah." He leaned back in the squeaky chair, wagging a finger at her as though the recent tension between them had never existed. "The Nick Bates case. Yes, Harry called and filled me in on your little conversation in the café. Wanted to know if I'd put you up to it. But, no, that was all you." He grinned proudly. "I must say, it's quite the riddle."

"It's just got more complicated," she said quietly.

"Joseph Smith was murdered. By the looks of it, he was stabbed and pushed down the stairs."

"What's your gut telling you?"

"That I have no clue what's going on." She laughed, if a touch sombrely. "Joey did *something*, and now he's dead. Agnes and Jeanie know what that *something* is. Gwyneth might. I feel like the pieces are all on the table, but I can't quite figure out the picture on the puzzle."

"Well, it sounds like your list of suspects might have just narrowed."

"To Agnes and Gwyneth?"

"And perhaps the brother, since he owed him a considerable sum." He paused before adding, "Perhaps even DI Ramsbottom, too. His dislike of Nick bordered on a vendetta. Although – and despite our family's abysmal track-record here – I can't imagine Harry going that far."

"Besides, what reason would he have to kill Joey?"

"And the two ladies have reasons?"

"Maybe?" She leaned her elbows onto her knees and rubbed at her temples. "Agnes is part of the club, so she could have been crossed by both men. Gwyneth had an on and off again thing where she basically traded one for the other for years – and now they're both dead."

"Black widow?"

"I don't think so." Claire shook her head. "What did she have to gain from killing Nick?" Her eyes lit up, and she sat bolt upright and clapped her hands together. "But what if 'what Joey did' was killing Nick? Then Gwyneth stabbed him and pushed him down the stairs in revenge for killing her true love?"

"It's certainly a nice theory, little one, but you'll have a hard time proving it," he said with a hearty chuckle. "Let's go back in. I can smell your mother's emergency lasagnes. I know she's always embarrassed to pull them out, but secretly? It's my favourite of all the things she makes."

"Mine too."

Claire linked arms with her father as they strolled up the garden path. She glanced up at her bedroom window on the way, finding she wasn't upset to be sticking around for a little while longer. Ryan needed her help, after all. Before they reached the back door, Claire heard a familiar hiss from over the fence. Leaving her father to go inside, she peered into Graham's back garden.

As expected, Domino was standing off against a black cat next to Graham's knocked-over bin. Though last night's storm had probably tipped it, she knew without a doubt Domino's had been the claws to rip open the bags. Despite being the slenderer and more innocent-looking of Claire's two cats, Domino's schemes to get more food never ceased. The other cat – one of Mrs Beaton's, she assumed, though she wasn't close enough to get a whiff – didn't stand a chance when there was a half-stripped chicken carcass on offer.

"*Domino?*" Claire growled, motioning for her to return to the appropriate side of the garden fence. "Are you trying to get us in trouble? Get over here."

But Domino wasn't listening. She growled deep in her throat at the black cat before hissing and swinging with claws outstretched. Domino didn't make contact, but he scurried off all the same. With deceptive elegance, Domino returned to picking at the chicken.

Knowing Domino wouldn't take her threats seriously with a barrier between them, Claire tiptoed down the side of her parents' cottage and hopped over the place where the fence lowered at the front. Ryan and his mother, Paula, had once lived in the house Graham now inhabited alone. It had been far too big for two and was definitely far too big for one.

Claire reached the kitchen window and ducked when she saw Graham washing something at the sink. Holding her breath, she crept along in a thigh-burning squat and snatched Domino up. The cat wriggled, but

Claire gripped her for dear life. She was about to pivot back but, in a sea of scrunched up beer cans, something bright and plastic caught her eye.

A red lid.

A red lid attached to a can of spray paint.

Claire didn't hesitate. She turned and hurried back under the window, standing when she could. With Domino still in her arms, she hopped over the wall and through the front door. She bumped straight into Ryan's back.

"Look at that for timing," he said, steadying her with a hand on her arm. "Ready to start on the furniture at the flat?"

"I know who sprayed my shop."

His eyes widened. "Who?"

Claire peered past him into the kitchen. Alan was chatting at the table with Sally as he tucked a napkin into his collar, and Janet had the kids on a stool at the sink, already washing their hands.

"It was my next-door neighbour," she said, glancing through the side window at the cottage. "It was Graham."

CHAPTER THIRTEEN

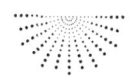

*A*fter lasagne and the kids' baths, Janet insisted on putting them to bed with a story – something they were both eager for. Claire wasn't sure they would be so keen after hearing one. Janet's thinly disguised village gossip spun into strange but boring fairy tales were about as interesting as reading the phonebook. Although, those stories had always sent Claire straight off to sleep, so perhaps her mother was actually a devious mastermind.

Neither in the mood for an early night, Ryan and Claire walked Sally home. She suggested a taxi, but Claire knew the fresh air would do her good before she stumbled home wine-drunk. When Sally was somewhat soberer and safely on the other side of her front door, Claire and Ryan strolled through the park to the square. The last of the sun had already slipped away by the time they reached the flat above the shop.

Ryan started taking the pieces out of their boxes while Claire made them strong cups of coffee in the small kitchen. Before taking them through to the bedroom, she glanced through the front window to the brightly up-lit clock tower in the square. Less than a week had passed since the opening. The nerves she'd had that first morning almost felt silly now, especially considering everything that had happened since. The electrics, mice, and tiles felt tame in comparison.

"I wonder if things would have played out differently if we'd somehow figured out it was Graham and not Nick," she said, setting the cups on the narrow window ledge. This view wasn't nearly as lovely, as the window looked out on nothing more than the dark alley behind the shops. "Would our paths have entwined with these murders? Would they just have been something we heard about through the gossips?"

"Probably," he said as he set the tufted, grey fabric headboard against the wall in the space where the double bed would most naturally fit. "Although, your uncle was technically still connected to Nick, and everything is out in the open with your dad now. Swings and roundabouts." He motioned for Claire to pick up the left side of the bed. "You really think

Graham would do that? I thought you were all cool after what happened with your uncle?"

"How could it ever be 'cool?'" she asked as he drilled in the screws. "My uncle murdered my neighbour's wife and his wife's lover. All this time, I've felt sorry for myself for having to keep up appearances with him, but . . . Graham is the real victim here. Well, the only one still left alive."

"He sprayed your shop, mate," Ryan said, arching a brow. "No matter what's happened, that's out of line."

"Maybe," she agreed, nodding her head from side to side. "Maybe it made him feel better."

"It made you feel awful."

"I got over it," she said, suddenly remembering the lift to the village. "And so did he, I think. He picked me up when it was raining and brought me to work. We talked, and even if he was a bit intense, he didn't seem to want to strangle me."

"Must have felt guilty. But, Claire, he owes you an apology, at least."

"It's done now." She held up the right side of the bed while Ryan glanced at the instructions and gathered the screws he needed. "This has gone up easier than I expected. I don't know why I was putting it off so long. Lucky I did, really, or I might already be in here."

"I still feel weird about this." His cheeks were red when he glanced up at her over the drill. "Can I give you some rent, at least? I was paying Agnes and Jeanie over four hundred a month. I can stretch to five-fifty, but the houses on the market 'round here start at six-fifty. And that's for the small ones."

"Then save your money," she said. "I don't need your money, Ryan. Like I said, it'd only be sitting empty, and you need it more than I do. I could have gone weeks before I started on this stuff."

They attached the bottom of the bed, and after rolling out the slats, the bed was up. Claire unwrapped the plastic covering the mattress, and Ryan made the bed better than Claire ever could. Her mother was so strict about how she liked the beds – which she made in every room every day –Claire had always been scared to try anything more than throwing her duvet up and down a few times. When Ryan finished smoothing the quilt over the fitted sheet, they lay down side by side and stared up at the textured ceiling and the bright domed light above them.

"Isn't this mad?" He rolled onto one side to face her as he spoke; she mirrored his movement. "After all these years, after all we've been through and all the changes, here we are. And it's still us, just like it used to be."

Claire tried to gulp around her suddenly parched throat.

"Just like we used to be," she said, glancing at his lips. "Ryan?"

"Yeah?"

"Do you ever think about what would have happened if you'd stayed?"

"All the time."

"And . . . what do you think?"

"Dunno," he said, rolling back to look at the ceiling. "I'd probably never have got in shape. Maybe wouldn't have had kids so young, not that I regret them. College? Maybe I would have followed my passion for art when the dust settled after my mum died. Who knows?" He glanced at her. "Is that what you meant?"

"Yeah," she lied, rolling off the other side and standing. "Like you said, who knows."

"Em keeps telling me not to regret things," he said, rising to join her. "'Live in the moment.' I always think I am, and then I look at the moment and realise I'm not. I'm so distracted with work and the kids and trying to find us a new home." He looked down and smiled before wiping the creases out where he'd laid. "This is going to sound cheesy."

"Go on, I like cheesy."

"Sometimes I think the only time I really live in the

moment is when I'm with you," he said, scratching the back of his head as his brows reached for his hairline. "You make me feel like myself. A 'myself' I don't think I took to Spain." He paused and stared at the floor before his eyes shot up to meet Claire's. " I-I really missed you, and I didn't even realise it until I came home."

Claire smiled, touched more than she knew how to express. In the months since his return, she'd felt them slowly opening up and figuring each other out after their years apart. Still, tonight the flower of their friendship fully blossomed again. And as she stared at him, still in his gym clothes and looking nothing like the Ryan she remembered, she knew, just like she'd known when they were teenagers, exactly how she felt about him.

She still loved him.

She loved him in a way she had never loved anyone before.

"I missed you, too," was all she could bring herself to say. "Shall we crack on with the bedside cupboards?"

"Why not?" He picked up one of the boxes with the picture of the mid-century white and light-oak style cupboards she had chosen. "When we're done, a pint at the pub before last orders."

The race to get to The Hesketh Arms for a pint of

homebrew before closing pushed them through the two bedside tables at lightning speed. They even had time to slash the plastic off the small, L-shaped corner sofa she'd picked for the open-plan living and kitchen area at the front of the flat.

"Kids can have the bed," Ryan said, sitting on the soft grey fabric couch as Claire's phone vibrated in her pocket. "I don't mind crashing on here. Pillows and a quilt and I won't know the difference. Might even be comfier than the beds at the B&B. I spent most nights counting the springs in my back, not sheep."

Claire opened her phone to find a text message from Sally: *Might be the wine talking, but I just realised your uncle's cottage is bang in Ryan's price range and has three bedrooms. Dunno when it's going on the market after Joey's tumble, but it shouldn't take too long. Could probably even negotiate a discount. Double murder site ... too weird?*

Without even thinking about her response, Claire sent back a quick two-word text: *Too weird*.

"Pub?" she said.

"Pub."

After flicking off the lights, they went downstairs and out through the front door. Claire locked up and turned to see Damon walking towards them from the direction of his flat above Marley's Café, a box of toffee apple cider in his hand.

"Looks like I'm too late," Damon said, patting the small case. "Saw your light on and assumed you were flatpacking again."

"We were," she said, looping arms with Ryan on one side and Damon on the other. "And now the three of us are off to the pub for a pint before closing."

"What about these?" He held up the cider.

"Stuff them under your jacket," she said. "Like I said, a pint before closing. Those'll do us nicely on a bench in Starfall Park when Malcolm and Theresa kick us out."

"Drinking on a park bench?" Damon grumbled. "Like a bunch of delinquent teenagers?"

"Less of the delinquent," Ryan called across. "We used to call ourselves 'cool,' thank you very much. Don't knock it till you've tried it, mate."

The three of them laughed as they approached the pub, but the laughter quickly faded when they spotted the lone occupant of the outside beer garden. In the middle of a sea of benches, Gwyneth stared blankly into a glass of white wine. Her red lipstick was merely a smudged stain, and the eyeliner had gone, washed away with tears by the looks of it. Without her trademark make-up, Gwyneth was a shadow of Northash's Marilyn.

"Gwyneth?" Claire said softly as she approached. "I

was sorry to hear about your loss. I know you were close to Joey."

"Hmmm?" She didn't look up from the wine. "Oh, yes, Joey. Thank you, honey."

Gwyneth finally summoned part of a shaky smile and glanced up, but the expression didn't touch her eyes. The pain of her recent losses was etched in every line of her face. Though Northash residents called her 'Marilyn,' Claire didn't think anyone could fake such a blank and harrowing stare into nothingness.

"He stopped my brother going to prison for a silly drunken scuffle," Damon offered with a meek smile. "Good lawyer."

"No, he wasn't," Gwyneth replied, her lips twitching into a smile. "He was a terrible lawyer. No moral compass. But, then, Mum always said I had terrible taste in men." She picked up the glass and sipped it for what seemed like the first time. "At least Nick knew he was no good. He always said I was too good for him. We met at my twenty-year school reunion." She paused, her smile widening. "He came with Ste. I'd never seen him before, but there he was, dancing in the middle of the empty dance floor with a bottle of beer in his hand. No shame, no embarrassment, just dancing. He didn't care who was watching. He didn't know anyone there but his brother, but even if he had, he wouldn't have cared. That was the type of man he was." She paused to smile. "I think I fell in love with him before we'd even said two words to each other. Under it all, he was *good*." She dabbed away a tear. "Joey thought being a lawyer made him a good man, but he screwed over so many more people, just in a different way. The people he *knew* were guilty . . . and he fought to let them walk free. It turns my stomach. If we hadn't known each other since childhood, I would have dropped him years ago. It's hard to see who someone has become when all you can think about is who they used to be. The list of people who would want to murder either of them could be as long as my arm."

"And yet I'm sure the list of people who would want to murder them *both* is a much smaller one," Claire said, sitting across from Gwyneth. "Do you have any ideas who that could be?"

Gwyneth shook her head. "He came to my shop right before he died. He seemed spooked. I asked him what was wrong, and he said he'd done something terrible but that he could never tell me about it. Said I needed plausible deniability – those were his words. And then he went off to meet someone. If I'd known he was going to . . . I could have . . ."

"Don't blame yourself," she said quietly. "Take it

from me, that gets you nowhere. Did he say who he was going to meet?"

Gwyneth shook her head again. "He called someone. Told them to meet at the usual place. I had a feeling it was the casino. We all had keys for the back door. Your uncle trusted us, but Nick . . . he ruined everything. It got out of control, and they couldn't stop. Investing and reinvesting, winning more and more. Gambling more and more."

"Who?"

"Nick and Joey," she said, grimacing into the calm surface of her chilled wine. "Nick always loved betting on the dogs and horses. Reckoned he had a fool-proof system for guessing winners. Worked just about enough times for people to fall for it but he'd never take my money. I knew then that it was just luck. People would place bets, Nick would let them win big at the casino, and then he'd convince them to reinvest their winnings into his races pool. The more money he had to play with, the more chances he had to make it back. For a while, it worked. But it all got too big."

"What happened?" Claire pushed, edging forward on the bench.

"About a week before he died," she said, blinking hard and freeing more tears, "he lost it all. The entire kitty. He paid out the profits every month, like a business investment, but he burned through the lot. He said he just kept losing and losing, and before he knew it, it was all gone."

"How much?" Ryan asked, slipping next to Claire on the bench.

"Twelve thousand pounds." She looked up at the sky and blew a steady stream of air through her pursed lips. "He was so stupid. He said the bookies kept throwing him out, so he kept going to different ones to try and win it back. Everyone was furious with him. I knew it would happen eventually. He didn't care about winning money to pay people back; he just cared about having money to play with." She drank more wine and shivered, though from the alcohol or her thoughts, Claire couldn't tell. "Joey, on the other hand, cared about the money. After a lifetime struggling as a lawyer, he got his first taste of what he called 'real cash.' He hated Nick, but the money was good enough for him to join the club. Uncle Harry says there's a chance their deaths aren't connected, what with the methods being so different. Nick was strangled with a rope, and Joey was stabbed in the neck."

"So, he *was* stabbed," Claire said, almost to herself.

"Blunt instrument, Harry said." She closed her eyes as though to stop more tears. "He said it looked like a fencing blade or maybe even a pen. It went deep enough that he would have died even without being pushed down—" Her hand went up to her mouth. "I . . . I should go home."

"We'll walk you," Claire offered.

"No, no, it's alright." Gwyneth wiped her tears as she shuffled to the end of the bench. "I only live in the flat above my shop." She rested a hand on Claire's shoulder. "You were right about your candle. It really filled the whole room. Welcome to the square, Claire."

When Gwyneth was safe inside her flat, Claire turned her gaze across the square to take in her candle shop, enjoying the fluttering in her tummy.

"It's still surreal," she said.

"I've heard nothing but good things," Ryan said, nudging her arm slightly. "Let's get that pint before they lock up."

Inside The Hesketh Arms, the worn-out and dated décor proved a comfort after that devastating conversation with Gwyneth. A couple of men propped up the bar, and despite the late hour, Malcolm and Theresa, the owners, were still smiling.

"On me," Claire announced, reaching for her purse. "I need to spend my money on something now that I'm a small business owner."

Ryan and Damon drifted to the table in the corner, which was where Claire drank with each of them whenever she visited. Seeing them get along so easily was a relief. She'd worried she'd have another Sally and Damon situation on her hands; feeling like she needed to keep her friends separate was awful.

"Three pints of homebrew, is it, Claire?" Theresa asked, already reaching for the clean glasses. "How's the shop going? I've meant to get over to show my face, but you know what it's like. We're married to this place."

"Gladly," Malcolm said, kissing his wife on the cheek as he passed. "I've been seeing your little flame bags all week. We knew you'd pull it off."

"I'm glad *you* did," she joked. "But thank you, I really appreciate that. I'll drop off a bag of samples tomorrow."

"That's very sweet of you." Theresa put the first pint of dark Hesketh Homebrew onto the brass plate on the bar. "I do like a candle with a bubble bath."

Claire reached into her bag to grab her purse. The thought of a bubble bath was an enticing one. She'd been so busy in the months leading to the shop opening, she'd only had time to grab showers – and not even her usual long ones, at that. After rounding off the stressful day with her friends and a drink, maybe she'd remedy that when she got home. She paid and carried all three pints over at once, only spilling a little as she settled them onto the circular dark wood table.

"Do you think Gwyneth did it?" Damon asked after sipping his beer. "News travelled up the hill just before the end of our shift, and that's what everyone was saying. She's a clear link between the two men."

"But not the only link," Claire pointed out, the bitter homebrew familiar and comforting on her tongue. "I thought the same, though, until just now."

"You believed it, too?" Ryan asked as he picked up his pint. "She seemed broken."

"Yeah, she did." Damon yawned and pushed up his glasses. "Who else is on your list of suspects, Claire?"

Claire stared at the reflection of the light on the wall through the shiny surface of the table. Something itched in the back of her mind like a bug bite she couldn't quite scratch.

"A fencing blade," Damon said when she didn't reply. "That was a bit weird, don't you think? Who even fences these days?"

"*Like* a fencing blade," Claire pointed out, a penny dropping in her mind as the words left her lips. "There are other blunt, pointed instruments."

"Like what?" Ryan asked.

"Like a knitting needle." Claire's stomach lurched. "That would do it."

"Knitting needle?" Ryan's eyes widened. "*Oh*."

The penny landed on the floor of her mind with a deafening thud. More pennies followed, clattering and reverberating as pieces of information fell into place.

"Who are you talking about?" Damon asked.

"Agnes," Ryan answered. "I think. Surely not?"

"Why not?" Claire asked with a shrug. "Her name was there in the guestbook. You never know what someone is capable of. We're all only one decision away from ruining our lives." She stood so suddenly she knocked the top off her pint, but she couldn't stay to drink it. "I think we need to get to the B&B."

Claire ran for the door, but before her hands touched the wood, she spun and redirected herself to the bar. Ryan and Damon skidded to a halt right behind her, diverting themselves. Claire leaned against the bar, looking through the open door at the back of the pub. Malcolm wasn't there, but Theresa, with a jaw-cracking yawn, was refilling a box with bags of crisps. She caught Claire's eye on the tail end and pushed forward a smile, too perfect a host to let her tiredness show.

"Surely not another so fast?" Theresa asked with a chuckle. "You must have had a hard day."

"Something like that," Claire said, glancing at their

table. "We've actually got to go. I just wanted to ask you something."

"Go ahead."

"My uncle's casino," she said, cutting straight to the point. "I heard you and Malcolm were part of it?"

Theresa's smile faltered for a brief second before she picked up a cloth and dragged it over the already sparkling bar.

"We were," she replied in a quieter voice. "We left, though."

"When Nick took over?"

Theresa nodded. "It was a bit of fun, at first, but they kept driving up the stakes. I was surprised anyone stuck around."

"Was Agnes one of them?"

"Oh, she *loved* it," Theresa whispered, glancing at the two half-asleep men propped up at the end of the bar in front of their almost-drained pints. "Greedier than I ever thought, that one. Nothing like her sister, is she?"

"That she's not." Claire slapped the bar and pushed away. "Thanks, Theresa. We need to go."

They left the pub, setting off across the quiet square under the golden glow of the streetlamps – first at a walk, then a fast walk, and finally a sprint. With no rain to slow them, they reached the B&B in less than a minute.

"I've lived with the woman for months," Ryan said. "Being grumpy is one thing, but murder?"

"She wasn't just grumpy though, was she?" Claire wasted no time running up the stairs before turning and adding, "You saw her dragging Amelia up the stairs. And Jeanie's cheek?"

Claire opened the front door and headed straight down the hallway without pausing. She followed the sound of weeping. In the sitting room, Jeanie was crying in the corner, clutching her wrist and rocking back and forth. Claire rushed over and wrapped an arm around the hysterical woman.

"Did Agnes do this?" Claire asked.

"I think it's broken," she said through hiccoughed breaths.

"Jeanie, did your sister do this to you?"

She nodded, letting go of her wrist to roughly wipe away her tears with her uninjured hand. "She's always had our father's nasty streak."

Claire helped Jeanie up off the floor and into her rocking chair. Next to it, a basket of wool sat on a side table, various knitting needles stabbed into the balls.

"Get her something cold from the kitchen," Claire instructed Ryan. "Damon, go with him."

The two of them went without a fuss, and when Claire was alone with Jeanie, she perched on the edge of the coffee table and held the woman's unhurt hand between both of hers.

"I see it in your eyes," Claire said, offering a supportive squeeze. "I've seen that look in the mirror in my own eyes. You know what Agnes did, don't you? You know she murdered Nick and Joey?"

Jeanie could only nod before the wailing started afresh. Ryan rushed in with a bag of frozen cauliflower wrapped in a tea towel. He handed it to Claire, who placed it gently on Jeanie's swollen wrist where the skin was hot to the touch.

"She gambled *everything*!" Jeanie cried through her sobs. "Every penny we had ever made from this place, she fed into that stupid club! She kept winning enough to keep the debt collectors at bay, but she was obsessed with the idea of making enough to get rid of all of our debt. She really believed it was going to work. She said women our age shouldn't have so much debt hanging over them. I wanted her to focus on the B&B, maybe advertising in a travel magazine, but she was convinced Nick could win her what she needed. 'He's done it before, and he'll do it again' she kept saying."

"How much did he win her?"

"A little over four thousand," Jeanie said, stumbling

over the number. "Enough to pay off a quarter of the mortgage left on this place, but it wasn't enough for her. She fed it all back in, and he lost it all. Every penny. He said he'd sort it, but how could he? I left the club when things got too serious, but Agnes? She just couldn't give it up – another thing she inherited from our father." Through a sad smile, Jeanie told Ryan, "If you hadn't paid us so consistently, we'd have shut down long ago. You've been our only regular source of income."

Claire thought back to Jeanie's remark about them being their only guests when they'd left the sisters to babysit Amelia and Hugo the night of Claire's surprise party. Agnes had been indifferent to them, but Jeanie had seemed so eager to bend over backwards. Though she'd sensed some unrest between the sisters then, she would never have guessed how deep their rift ran.

"Where's Agnes now?" Claire asked, looking up at the ceiling. "Is she here?"

"No." Jeanie pulled the tea towel from the frozen veg and rubbed her eyes with it. "She came home covered in blood. God, there was so much blood." Her bottom lip wobbled. "She went for a bath, and then packed us each a suitcase and proclaimed that we were leaving Northash. When I refused, she tried to drag me." She glanced at her wrist. "I think it is broken."

"Where did she go?" Ryan asked.

"She said she was going to catch a train." Jeanie rested her head against the back of the rocking chair and closed her eyes. "I don't know which station."

"What's the nearest?" Claire asked.

"Looking," Damon said, already on his phone. "Clitheroe Interchange. No running trains until morning. Nearest station with any departing trains is Preston, and it looks like there's an hour wait until any of them set off."

"How far is Preston in a car?"

"About forty minutes," Damon answered. "Could be quicker this time of night."

"When did she leave?"

"About half an hour ago." Jeanie looked at the ornate clock on the mantelpiece. "Give or take."

"Call yourself an ambulance for that wrist," Claire instructed as she stood. "We need to get to Preston station."

"There's still one taxi running," Damon revealed, tapping on his phone. "This new app is marvellous. Shall I book it?"

"No," she said, already heading to the door. "It'll be quicker if we run to the rank."

Once again, they sprinted through the square, up past the post office, and straight into the Northash

Taxi rank. Through the small window in the wall between the waiting area and office, Claire saw Ste with a headset wrapped around his neck. To Claire's surprise, Em was cross-legged on the counter behind him, a creased paperback in her lap, folded at the spine.

"*Claire?*" Em grinned, sliding off the counter and marking her page with a fold in the corner. "What a nice surprise. Are you three off on a little night out? Canal Street in Manchester will just about be getting going at this time. Cheap drinks mid-week, too."

"As tempting as that sounds, not tonight," she replied, her breath shaky from the running and the shock. "We need to get to Preston station immediately."

"Another one?" Ste arched a brow as he pulled off his headset. "Just had one of them sisters from the B&B waiting about fifteen minutes for a taxi to take her. Tapped her foot the whole bloody time. Was driving me up the wall."

"Count yourselves lucky that's all she did," Claire said, looking back at Ryan and Damon before turning back to Ste and saying, "I think she killed your brother and Joey. And if we don't get to the station now, she might just get away with it."

"Then I guess I'm driving." Ste leaned forward and snatched a set of keys from the wall. "Car's out front."

They piled into the blue car with the Northash Taxi sticker on the side. Once Claire was sandwiched between Damon and Ryan in the backseat, she realised it was the same cab they'd taken back from Manchester.

"I'm going to kill her," Ste said, his calm voice a contrast to his words as he tugged his seatbelt across his stomach and chest. "Don't let me near her, Em, because I will kill her."

"Let's just focus on driving." Em patted his hand as he pushed down the handbrake and eased the car away from the kerb. "One turn at a time."

Ste turned the lights on, illuminating the park entrance. The back of a bright pink dressing gown with white and gold trim caught Claire's eye, and she knew who it belonged to before the occupant turned around. Sally spun at the sudden flare of light, holding a plastic bag from the late-night tiny chain supermarket on the other side of the roundabout. She leaned forward and squinted before rushing to the edge of the street to wave her arms.

"Can you stop?" Claire instructed Ste, leaning over Damon to wind down the window before shouting, "I thought we took you home."

"Fancied ice cream." Sally peered into the car, her gown opening enough to reveal that she was, thankfully, wearing pyjamas. "You're not off on a night out without me, are you?"

"Better," Damon replied, pushing up his glasses. "We're off to confront a murderer."

"Which is why we need to go," Claire said, smiling her apology as she checked the clock in the dashboard. "Sorry, Sally, we—"

"Not without me, I don't think." Sally ripped open the door and clumsily climbed in, cramming herself onto Damon's lap. "Paul won't even notice I've gone." She awkwardly closed the door behind her, head bent at an uncomfortable angle against the fabric ceiling. She pulled a tub of strawberry cheesecake ice cream from the bag, and said, "Don't suppose anyone has a spoon?"

CHAPTER FOURTEEN

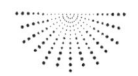

They followed the road along the bottom wall of Starfall Park until it gave way to the A-roads of the countryside. These soon turned to B-roads, and after a little congestion at a large roundabout thanks to a slip road being closed for roadworks, they finally broke free onto the motorway.

Once Ste reached the same speed as the few cars dotted along the quiet stretch, he overtook them and kept speeding until the g-force dragged Claire backwards into the middle seat. She comforted herself by mentally repeating that if anyone could speed safely, it was a taxi driver. The mantra might even have worked if she didn't see Em's hand darting to Ste's knee to give it a gentle squeeze when the speed dial crept past ninety miles per hour. He slowed down a little, but his erratic weaving without indicating had blaring horns following them all the way down the motorway.

No one spoke.

No one dared.

Even Sally, so drunk that she had no problem sitting on Damon's lap in a dressing gown and licking the surface of a tub of ice cream like a cat, picked up on the tension in the air and didn't say a word. If Claire hadn't watched Sally polish off a bottle and a half of wine to herself following her shock discovery on the casino stairs, she would have insisted Ste pull over to let someone else drive. As it turned out, minus the drunk, they didn't have a licence between them.

Thankfully, just when Claire was sure she couldn't take another second of fearing for her life, the motorway ended in a large roundabout. Not long afterwards, they were in a built-up residential area and heading into Preston. Forced to finally slow down, it felt like they were crawling, but a quick glance at the clock let Claire know they'd easily shaved ten minutes from the time the journey usually took.

The roundabouts and residential areas continued until they reached the familiar wide road towards the centre of the city. On either side of the road, groups of young adults strolled in the dark. The ones walking towards the city were laughing and joking, and the ones walking away were in states like Sally's. The edge of the bustling centre came up, but they turned right down a steep road that led straight to the grand entrance of the station. All their seatbelts unclicked before the car ground to a halt, perfectly centred in a parking space despite the swift stop.

Sally lumbered out first, helped with Damon's awkward shoving. Claire climbed out of Ryan's side, and they set off to the entrance. More young people loitered around the station entrance. One girl leaned against the wall in a short dress, shoes clutched in one hand, sobbing into her mobile phone. Two guys kissed on the other side, and another guy and girl argued in slurred shout-whispers as they walked back up the steep hill. Claire sometimes wondered what she'd missed not going to university.

"I think I'm—" Sally ran to the edge of the small, walled-in car park with her hand over her mouth. She bent over, and the wine and ice cream came back up.

"I'll stay with her," Damon said with a waft of his hand. "That car ride was enough adventure for one day."

With Sally and Damon waiting outside, they rushed through the bright ticket office and straight into the giant, open-air station. Obviously built in the

Victorian era, the sheer scale of the exposed-steel roof always took Claire's breath away. Matching steel walkways spread in either direction from the central platform, and they went down to two more long-reaching platforms on either side. The station was massive, and Claire couldn't see Agnes.

"We go in twos," Claire instructed, remembering her father's advice about never deploying lone officers. "We'll each check a side of the central platforms, and then Ryan and I will take the right side, and you two take the left. There are underground walkways at the bottom."

"What about the police?" Em asked. "Shouldn't we call someone to let them know what you've figured out?"

"Let's just see if Agnes is here first," Claire said, eyes consciously scanning the large space. "We could be too late."

With that, they went straight down the extended central platform, splitting at the row of shops and toilets right in the middle. Drunk youths were dotted around the place in small clusters, most worn-out and droopy as they waited for a late-night train home. There was a parked train on one of the right platforms, and another on the left side of the centre, but the train to Leeds wasn't due to leave for another ten minutes, and the train to Blackpool North for another twenty.

"She's not on this one," Ryan said after running to the bottom and back again. "Can't see her on the other side either. Should we check the bathrooms?"

"Worth a try." Claire watched as Em and Ste ran into the underground tunnel. "Why do I have a feeling she's not here?"

"I don't know," Ryan said, exhaling heavily as he looked around the cavernous station, "but I have the same feeling."

They walked down the brightly lit tiled corridor to the large bathrooms. The bathroom itself was empty, although one of the cubicles was occupied. From the loud vomiting, she doubted either of the two sets of high-heeled feet under the door belonged to Agnes. She left the bathroom and went back into the corridor. Ryan wasn't there, but a young, scrawny, bespectacled man was leaning against the wall like his life depended on it. He squinted at Claire, his neck bopping this way and that.

"What're you studying?" he asked.

"I'm not a student," she replied, unable to hold in her laughter. "I'm flattered, though."

He squinted again, his bending and wobbly knees snapping back to attention one at a time. If her mother saw such a sight, she'd have declared the boy a menace and a drunk, but Claire had been there many times, usually with Sally.

"You don't look old," he said. "Where're you going after here?"

Claire chuckled. She'd heard that chat-up line in nightclubs before, but never outside the toilets in a train station.

"I think I'm technically old enough to be your mother," she said, before doing the mental calculation and adding, "*just*."

"Nah," he said, staggering side to side, his finger extended. "You're my age. I can tell."

The ladies' bathroom door opened, and the two girls from the cubicle came out. One was struggling to walk; at least the other appeared sober enough to look after her. Claire had been both of those girls, although she hadn't been the one with mascara-streaks down her cheeks for a long while.

"*Mikey!*" the drunker of the two girls cried to the skinny lad, falling into him, and then using him to prop herself up. "Who's your friend?"

The other girl smiled her apologies at Claire, clearly embarrassed by the drunkenness of her friends. They couldn't have been twenty yet, but from the stories Sally told about university life, they weren't doing anything too out of the ordinary.

"She reckons she's old enough to be my mum," Mikey said.

The drunk girl squinted at Claire and said, "Nah. My mum's well older than that. You want to come to a house party?"

Ryan came out of the men's bathroom, shaking water off his hands. He stopped in his tracks when he saw the teenagers talking to Claire.

"Apparently, I'm passing for a teenager these days and being invited to parties." Claire winked at Ryan. "You took your time."

"Needed to go."

"Is this your boyfriend?" the drunk girl slurred. "He's well fit. Mikey, you should join the gym."

"C'mon," Claire said, nodding towards the opening of the corridor back into the station, "let's keep looking for her."

"Who you looking for?" the drunk girl asked, staggering as she tried to focus on Claire and indirectly blocking the entrance. "We lost our friends too. Three of them. Dunno where they went."

"Not a friend," Claire said, moving the girl politely to one side, "but if you see someone who looks like they'd murder you with a knitting needle, do come and find me."

With the girl out of the way, Claire hurried down the corridor and back onto the platform. A rowdy group of lads in polo shirts and tight jeans roared into the train hall, jumping around and chanting like they'd just come from a football match.

"Sometimes I don't feel grown-up," Claire said, scanning the platform in the opposite direction for any sign of Agnes, "and then I spend two minutes with *actual* teenagers and realise how much of an adult I am."

"At least you're not going to have to relive it," he said. "Hugo I'm not so worried about, but can you imagine Amelia at their age? I don't think I'll ever be ready."

As Claire turned in the direction of the underground walkway, a finger tapped meekly on her shoulder. She turned, surprised to see the only of the trio who wasn't blind drunk. Mikey and the girl were snogging against the tiles; Claire hoped she'd brushed her teeth, somehow.

"Were you joking about the woman?" the girl asked, wrapping her arms around herself. "Only because I saw one waiting on the train and she was knitting."

"No, I'm not joking," Claire said seriously. "Which train?"

"Blackpool North."

Claire turned and looked at the train on Platform 4 to the right side of the station. She'd scanned the windows on her search, and she hadn't seen Agnes. She couldn't see her now, either, and was about to accept defeat when she spotted the rectangle gaps on either side of the carriage where more windows could fit.

A deeply buried memory pushed its way to the surface.

"Let's get a closer look."

With Ryan by her side, they jogged down the platform to the opening of the underground walkways. An ornate red and green railing guided them down below the station. The lower corridors, with their bare white walls and too bright lighting, were a stark contrast to the station above. As they'd done in the square earlier, they set off on a pace that began as a walk and soon increased to a jog. By the time they were at the top of the staircase on the other side of the tracks, they were running.

And there Agnes was.

Alone in an empty carriage.

In the only seat without a window.

Claire had been on the Blackpool North train many times in her life, but she must have been nine or ten in the memory that had sprung forward. They'd all gone as a family, changing at Preston station to get as close to Northash as they could. Exhausted from a fun day at the seaside, all Claire had wanted to do was rest her head against the window and watch the English countryside whiz by. When she'd sat down, she'd been devastated to see a plastic panel with no window. Without even needing to ask, Uncle Pat swapped seats with her, and she got her wish. However, she was sure she'd fallen asleep within minutes of the train setting off anyway.

"She really *is* knitting," Ryan said with a disbelieving laugh. "What do we do?"

Claire set off without giving it a second thought. When she hadn't been worrying about Ste's driving, she'd been thinking about what she'd say to Agnes if they found her. Now that Agnes was in her sights, lumpy long brown knitting creation and all, every word left Claire's mind. Still, she marched onto the bright train and took the seat opposite Agnes.

"I see my sister really doesn't have a shred of loyalty in her body," Agnes said bitterly, her fingers forcefully twisting the wool around the needles. "Of all the people, why did it have to be *you*?"

Agnes glared at Claire with hatred she was all too familiar with. Claire had seen the same hatred in Agnes' eyes every time she'd vocally opposed Claire's desire to rip out the old tearoom. She hadn't been the only one, but Agnes had been the ringleader.

"And here I was thinking things were okay between us," Claire said as sarcastically as she could. "I know what you did."

"*No?* You don't say," Agnes fired back, her tone matching Claire's as she shifted the wool creation to the opposite needle to start a fresh row. "And here I thought you were off on a little holiday to Blackpool at midnight. I suppose you want to know why?"

"I already know why," she replied quickly. "Took me a while to figure it out, I'll admit that, but I got there in the end. Did you want the money so badly?"

"They promised to triple it." The needles continued to work. "Quadruple it. And they did. They kept doing it. Every time, they gave me more money than I gave them, so I went all in." Her lip curled. "Joey promised the money was as good as mine. All I had to do was trust them. He might have hated the man, but he believed in Nick's magical gambling powers. I believed it too."

"When something sounds too good to be true," Claire said, "it probably is."

"Oh, what do *you* know?" Agnes forced a laugh, her needles stilling. She stared Claire dead in the eyes. "When people like *you* fall on your backsides, you have your lovely middle-class parents to pick you up. My parents are dead, and I'm glad of it. Nothing in this life was handed to me. Everything I have, I laboured for. That B&B, we struggled for it, and look how it treated us. Where did the guests go?" She jabbed at her knitting, even more aggressively; the needles started to sound like fencing blades, a little. "To the chain hotels! And we had to count on *him*," she said, pausing to nod at Ryan in the train's doorway, "and his horrible brats to keep the roof over our head? Jeanie wasn't going to fix it, so I had to. Nick taking over that club finally gave me the chance. My dad always said, 'Gamble big, or don't bother.' Nick won us twelve thousand pounds! Four grand each! But it wasn't enough, so we went all in again. Nick swore he'd make us even more."

"And he lost it."

"Every damn penny," she said through gritted teeth. "I gave him a day to make it back. Borrowed money off his brother, and what did the idiot do? Lost it all. He could have given me *that* money, but he—"

"Didn't owe it to you," Claire cut in. "It's called gambling for a reason."

"He *promised*," Agnes growled. "*They* promised.

Joey was a lawyer! I *trusted* him." She inhaled deeply. "I went to see Nick, but I knew he wouldn't have the money. I *knew* it. That's why I took the rope. He wasn't going to get away with it if he couldn't pay me."

"And you strangled him?"

"Big fella like that, you'd think it would have been difficult," she said with a sigh. "Didn't even struggle. It's like he understood. Maybe he wanted it?"

"Or maybe he was exhausted from working out in the gym all morning?"

"Was like popping the head off a dandelion," Agnes continued, gazing right through Claire. "I didn't plan past that, though. It was just lucky that Joey had come 'round to see if Nick won the money back."

"*That's* what Joey did." Claire exhaled, sinking deeper into the chair. "He helped frame Nick's murder as a suicide."

"It was his idea," Agnes said with a dry half-smile. "He made it sound so easy. Took the both of us to get him up on that beam, but we did it. Should have known he didn't have the stones to handle it. A man who can't accept that he's balding never does." She paused, lowering her knitting, her wicked smile fixed on Claire. "He called and told me that *you*, of all people, knew what he'd done. I knew you were bluffing. Heard you asking Jeanie. Those old floors are as thin as paper."

"If you knew I was bluffing, why did you kill him?"

"Because he was weak. Spineless. He would have cracked. It was only a matter of time before he told his precious *Marilyn*." She rolled her eyes. "I met him at the cottage. He attacked me, but I never go anywhere without my knitting. I was surprised by how easily one of my little needles punctured the skin."

"And pushing him down the stairs?"

"I wanted to make sure I did the job properly," she said with a shrug. "But I also knew I wouldn't get away with it this time. Nick, maybe, but killing Joey too would send the police back to the casino. I thought I'd at least have time to make a run for it, and then *you* turn up out of the blue." Agnes looked Claire up and down, pursing her lips. "You know, when I heard you were taking over Jane's Tearoom, I actually thought you'd make a good job of it. I thought 'fat lass like that will know how to make a good cake.'"

"I'm only good at eating them," Claire fired back, not letting her face crack. "You're a bully, Agnes. I pity you. You've clearly been very hurt by someone."

A loud fight broke out on the central platform, catching Claire's attention. Sloppy punches flew as screams of protest came from all directions. From the looks of it, the rowdy group of lads had turned on each other. On the other side of the station, Claire saw Mikey and the two girls hiding behind a vending machine.

Claire looked back at Agnes just in time for the mad knitter to make a run for the door. She yanked the needle from the wool and brandished it at Ryan. She dove at him but pulled back before she made contact. Ryan jumped back all the same, giving her enough room to dart through the gap. Claire jumped up and chased after her.

Agnes dashed towards the metal walkway, but Claire was faster. She reached out and tugged on the shoulder of Agnes' knitted cardigan. Agnes spun and lashed out with the knitting needle like she was an explorer hacking away at untouched jungle. The thin needle struck the side of Claire's arm, sharp enough to break the skin.

Claire gasped, but Agnes simply smirked as she glanced down at the bleeding cut. Claire's hand struck Agnes' cheek, almost like a reflex, and she gasped again. Agnes laughed and touched her cheek, her smirk growing.

"So that's what that feels like to be slapped," she said, her tongue poking at a small cut in her lip; it must have banged a tooth. "You know, I smelt one of your candles. I don't know what all the fuss is about."

Agnes took the stairs two at a time before rushing across the top of the walkway. Claire watched her run down the stairs on the other side, the knitting needle brandished in her hand.

"Let me see," Ryan said, grabbing her arm. "Doesn't look too deep."

"It's just a scratch. I think I hurt her more than she hurt me."

"Good."

Em and Ste made their way across the opposite walkway, but Agnes reached the central platform before they did. She glanced at the fight, and Claire could tell she was trying to choose if she should run through the front entrance or down to the underground walkway to slip out the side door. Seemingly choosing the entrance, she turned as six uniformed officers hurried in. Five of them went straight to the group of lads savagely punching and kicking the daylights out of each other, but one officer, a young woman, noticed the old woman brandishing a knitting needle like a weapon. Agnes lunged, but the officer's training kicked in. Agnes was pressed up against the wall before the knitting needle had time to clatter to the floor.

"You might want to keep hold of her," Ste called, rushing down the stairs on the other side. "She murdered my brother!"

The officer cuffed Agnes, and before long, the old woman was loaded in the back of one of the riot vans with the fighting men. Claire was relieved when the officer claimed to know DI Ramsbottom, although it took Claire gesturing with her finger up to her hair for it to fully click.

"She confessed to it all," Claire said when the four of them were in the entrance hall alone. "She didn't have a shred of remorse. I'm sorry, Ste."

"He can rest now," he said, sniffling back tears as Em rested her head on his shoulder. "It's over. Let's go home."

Silently, they walked through the front doors as the riot vans drove off. On the floor to the right, Damon leant against the wall. Sally, head and arms tucked up against his lap, was fast asleep. He was stroking her hair, but he stopped when his eyes met Claire's.

"She slept through the whole thing," he said, accepting Claire's hand up as Ryan guided Sally into the back of the taxi. "What happened to your arm?"

"A crazy woman with a knitting needle," she said, forcing back a yawn. "Come on, let's go home. I'll explain on the way."

With Sally taking up most of the corner, and Damon taking the middle seat, Claire took Ryan's lap like Sally had with Damon. Ryan wrapped his arms around her and held them together with looped fingers. He didn't let go until the taxi pulled up outside Sally's large, detached house.

Claire helped Sally, still half asleep, into her silent, show-home perfect house. Not wanting to disturb the peace, she guided her friend through to the sitting room and settled her under a fur blanket on the cream leather sofa.

"I've always been jealous of Damon being friends with you," Sally murmured as Claire tucked her in, "but he's nice."

"I always told you he was."

"I forgot men could be nice." She rolled over into the sofa, pulling the blanket tight around her neck. "Night, Claire."

"Night, Sally."

Claire kissed her friend on the side of the head. By the time Claire fetched a glass of water and a bucket from the kitchen, Sally was back to the soft snoring that had been the soundtrack for most of the taxi journey. On her way out, she glanced up the staircase, wondering if Paul, Sally's husband, had even noticed that his wife had been gone for hours after leaving in her dressing gown.

With more space back in the taxi, Ryan shuffled into the middle seat, and Claire sandwiched herself next to him. As the taxi slowly drove down the steep Park Lane, Ryan's fingers wrapped around hers in the gap between them on the backseat.

Claire didn't know what it meant, if anything at all, but it did feel nice.

CHAPTER FIFTEEN

The weekend following Agnes' arrest saw Claire rushed off her feet at the candle shop from opening to closing. Everyone wanted to talk to the woman behind the B&B owner's unmasking; Claire's retelling of the events at the train station never failed to have people hanging on her every word.

Joey's family held the funeral in a church outside the village. Claire decided not to go, but she attended Nick's at Trinity Community Church if only to provide moral support for Gwyneth now that they were shop neighbours. Jeanie turned up too, despite the strange looks she knew she'd get. Claire had spoken with her long enough to gather she planned on selling up and moving away. Neither of them mentioned that Jeanie had clearly kept her sister's murderous ways a secret. The woman had already lost enough. For different reasons, they skipped Nick's wake.

By the time Claire opened on Monday morning, with her father by her side, she was down to her last box of coconut milk candles for the 'Star Candle of the Month' display. When her mother walked in bang at noon, only two remained on the circular unit in the middle of the shop. Though Claire planned on making more, her mind had already turned to the puzzle of next month's Star Candle. She wasn't entirely sure what it would be but knew she wanted something floral.

"You two should get going now," Janet instructed, taking her place behind the counter. "They might not let you in if you're late."

But Claire and her father pulled up outside HM Prison Manchester with time to spare. They held hands and waited in silence until the crowd of visitors started flowing through the front door.

"Nice to see you again," the friendly woman from her previous visit said when they were in the queue at the desk. "Glad we didn't scare you off."

The woman behind the desk was just as snappy, but Claire wasn't nervous this time, so she seemed less frightening. She and her father went through security together, and it wasn't long until they were in the little holding pen with the windows into the visiting room. Alan kept his eyes glued to the floor, but this time, Claire looked inside. She saw Pat.

He waved.

She waved back.

The door buzzed and she entered, but her father remained behind.

"Isn't he coming?" Pat asked as Claire sat across from him.

"We're swapping at halftime," she said, glancing back at her father. "Guards said it wouldn't be a problem. There are some things a daughter shouldn't witness, and this is one of them." She pulled the envelope of photographs from her pocket and slid them across the table. "Said this wouldn't be a problem either. They're from your cottage. I didn't know what to do with them."

Pat pulled out the photographs and flicked through them, his smile growing with each familiar image. The final one was the picture of Pat and Nick in Vegas.

"Trip of a lifetime," he said, smiling fondly. "You should make sure to go, at least once."

Claire thought about mentioning the fact that the trip had unintentionally started the ball rolling for the deaths of Nick and Joey. Still, in the same way she and her family weren't responsible for Pat's mistakes, he wasn't accountable for Agnes'.

He didn't need another burden.

"I'm sorry, Uncle Pat," she said, able to look at him now. "I'm sorry for accusing you of having my shop sprayed. I shouldn't have jumped to conclusions."

"You have nothing to be sorry for," he replied, flicking through the pictures until he landed on the shot of them together by the sea. "I had an uncle once. Your gran's brother, Jacob. Uncle Jack, we called him. He died before you were born, but your father and I loved him like we did our own father. If he'd done what I did, I'd never be able to reconcile it. The fact you're here is enough for me." He paused and looked up at her with a tight smile. "Will I see you again?"

"Let's see how things go."

"That's good enough for me," he said, glancing at the large clock on the wall. "Now, there are ten minutes left before you swap, so I want to hear all about this candle shop of yours."

Claire spent the next ten minutes indulging him with every detail. The perfect image she'd once had of her uncle no longer existed, but he was still Pat, mistakes and all. She wasn't sure how often she'd write or visit, but she couldn't abandon him forever. He'd leave the prison in a body bag, and he knew that.

When the guard announced the halfway mark, she left him smiling, and that had to be enough.

"You've got this," she said to her dad as she passed him in the waiting room.

Claire kissed him on the cheek. Rather than lingering to watch, she waited outside, once again leaning against the wall under the hot sun. Ten minutes later, her father emerged, pale and with a shakier step than usual. Claire imagined she'd looked the same after her first visit, but she could already see her dad had pulled out the thorn. Whenever he got around to visiting again, it would be easier. He joined her against the wall and looked up at the sky.

"This place is punishing him enough," he said after a minute's silence. "He doesn't need it from us too."

"Mum won't mind watching the shop," Claire said, looping her arm through his and walking in the opposite direction of the parked car. "And I know a place where the drinks are cheap and the music is loud."

As they walked down the street, the hot summer sun above them, Claire knew the monster had been dragged out from under the bed, and she could barely remember why she'd been so scared of facing it in the first place.

After one raspberry vodka and lemonade each, they returned to the car and drove back to Northash. Claire took over behind the counter, and her parents stuck around, neither having anything else to do on a quiet Monday. By closing, Janet had organised all the receipts into a system even Claire vaguely understood, and which made more sense than stuffing them in a shoebox, and Alan had put together a bookcase in the flat above the shop.

Back at the cottage, Claire found Ryan in the garden. He'd set up two easels, and he and Amelia were on little stools, painting a landscape of the garden in front of them. Amelia's looked exactly as a nine-year-old's work would look, but Ryan's watercolour was so subtle and picturesque, Claire couldn't believe he'd ever doubt himself.

"Sally dropped this off earlier," Ryan said, slapping a file on the counter before walking over to fill up the kettle in the kitchen. "She thinks your uncle's cottage is the perfect fit for me."

"It is," Claire replied, deciding not to tell him she'd thrown Sally off the scent and then changed her mind and asked her to approach Ryan with the idea. "It has three bedrooms, it's slap bang in the middle of the village, and, now that all the furniture has been cleared out, it's ready and waiting."

Ryan made a face. "And two people were murdered there."

"Jane was murdered in my flat," she reminded him, grabbing a cup and setting it next to his. "Em and Ste will be back from their narrowboat trip next week. Get her 'round to sage the spirits away. Worked a treat in my place."

"And you're okay with it?"

"You need a house more than I need to be mad at my uncle," she said as he scooped coffee into the two cups. "Besides, how many houses do you know of that come with a casino in the basement?"

"Good point," he said with a laugh. "It would be nice for the kids to have their own rooms."

"Also comes with a cat," she said hopefully. "That's if you want Pickles? Sally has been feeding him every day, but he'll only go to the shelter if you say no."

"Nice subtle emotional blackmail there," he said with a badly concealed smile, peering into the garden at his daughter as she continued to paint alone. "Amelia did say she wanted a cat." He clapped his hands together. "Right, you've convinced me. I think I'll call Sally and get the ball rolling." He pulled his phone from his tight jeans. "And while I do that, go and change out of your good clothes. You're coming to paint with us, and I'm not taking no for an answer."

"*Good* clothes?" Janet remarked as she rushed into the kitchen and pulled a gammon joint out of the fridge. "I don't know how you can tell the difference, dear."

Leaving her mother to start on dinner and Ryan to call Sally, Claire hurried upstairs. In her bedroom, she was surprised to see Domino and Sid sniffing at a gift-wrapped oblong in the centre of her bed. There was a small tag, and she recognised the writing at once: *Had this finished for your opening, but I was a shy idiot. Hope you like it. R x*

Claire ripped back the paper, her heart fluttering. From the label, she knew it would be a painting, but when she saw the subject of it, she had to sit down on the edge of the bed to fully absorb it.

Ryan had created a delicate and beautiful rendition of the front of Claire's Candles in watercolour, complete with sign and summer window display. She rested the silver frame against her chest, and there she stayed until Domino and Sid's prowling around their food bowls tore her attention.

After feeding them and changing into some clothes she didn't mind covering in paint, Claire ran downstairs, only to be drawn to the front door by a repetitive banging. Across the garden fence, a young man was hammering a 'FOR SALE' sign into Graham's front garden while Graham watched on. He caught her eye and took a step back into the house.

Seconds later, he walked out, his hands deep in his pockets.

"*Claire?*" he called, walking up to the fence. "Can I have a word?"

"Sure."

Graham inhaled deeply, his eyes on the grass.

"I know," Claire said, deciding to spare him the embarrassment of having to confess. "I know you sprayed my shop."

"You do?" He shuddered. "Claire, I was drunk, and it was a moment of pure madness. I thought doing something . . . *anything* . . . I thought it would help, but it only made me feel worse. I wanted to tell you in the car, but I couldn't get the words out. I've been a coward."

"You've been human." She looked past him, towards the sign. "Moving somewhere nice, I hope?"

"I-I haven't decided yet." He frowned, clearly confused by Claire's dismissal of the graffiti. "I can't stay in this house, in this cul-de-sac. Too many ghosts. I need a fresh start where people don't have that look in their eyes."

"I know the look." She offered a sympathetic smile. "I hope you find that fresh start, Graham."

Inside, she passed the living room, doubling back when something new on the mantlepiece caught her eye. Or, rather, something old. Taped back together in four pieces, the Christmas morning, 1966, photograph of Alan and Pat had been placed back where it had always sat – exactly where it should be.

Despite what Pat had done, the happy memories were real, and that's all they had now.

"Thank you," Claire whispered to Ryan, kissing him on the cheek before sitting on the stool behind the easel he'd set up between them. "I love it."

Ryan blushed and smiled, simply continuing with his painting.

Under the clear blue sky, Radio Four drifted through her father's open shed door while her mother clattered in the kitchen. Even though another storm was forecast for that night, it was as perfect an evening as could be – and an excellent reminder of why Claire hadn't rushed to move into the flat above the shop just yet.

Claire glanced at Ryan as she made first contact with the paper with watery green paint. He gave her an encouraging nod, and her heart skipped a beat. She had to tell him how she felt, she knew that, but she had a painting to butcher.

She'd weather that storm another day.

For now, she would enjoy the sun.

I hope you enjoyed another trip to Northash! If you did, **DON'T FORGET TO RATE AND REVIEW ON AMAZON!**

Claire will be back for the 4th book in the series ROSE PETAL REVENGE November 30th 2020! Pre-order now for ONLY 0.99!

Thank you for reading!

DON'T FORGET TO RATE AND REVIEW ON AMAZON

I hope you enjoyed another visit to Northash!

Reviews are more important than ever, so show your support for the series by rating and reviewing the book on Amazon! Reviews are **CRUCIAL** for the longevity of any series, and they're the best way to let authors know you want more! They help us reach more people! I appreciate any feedback, no matter how long or short. It's a great way of letting other cozy mystery fans know what you thought about the book.

Being an independent author means this is my livelihood, and *every review* really does make a **huge difference**. Reviews are the best way to support me so I can continue doing what I love, which is bringing you, the readers, more fun cozy adventures!

Claire will be back for the 4th book in the series ROSE PETAL REVENGE November 30th 2020! Pre-order now for ONLY 0.99!

WANT TO BE KEPT UP TO DATE WITH AGATHA FROST RELEASES? *SIGN UP THE FREE NEWSLETTER!*

www.AgathaFrost.com

You can also follow **Agatha Frost** across social media. Search 'Agatha Frost' on:

Facebook
Twitter
Goodreads
Instagram

ALSO BY AGATHA FROST

Claire's Candles
1. Vanilla Bean Vengeance
2. Black Cherry Betrayal
3. Coconut Milk Casualty
4. Rose Petal Revenge (NEW!)

Peridale Cafe
Book 1-10 Boxset
1. Pancakes and Corpses
2. Lemonade and Lies
3. Doughnuts and Deception
4. Chocolate Cake and Chaos
5. Shortbread and Sorrow
6. Espresso and Evil
7. Macarons and Mayhem
8. Fruit Cake and Fear
9. Birthday Cake and Bodies
10. Gingerbread and Ghosts

11. Cupcakes and Casualties

12. Blueberry Muffins and Misfortune

13. Ice Cream and Incidents

14. Champagne and Catastrophes

15. Wedding Cake and Woes

16. Red Velvet and Revenge

17. Vegetables and Vengeance

18. Cheesecake and Confusion

19. Brownies and Bloodshed

20. Cocktails and Cowardice

21. Profiteroles and Poison

22. Pudding and Poison (NEW!)

Printed in Great Britain
by Amazon